# The Body and Blood

## A Parish Community

By: Deidre McVey

The Body and Blood

Copyright © August 2023 Deidre McVey
All rights reserved.

**In the spirit of the resurrection, this book is dedicated in loving memory of my stepfather.**

## CONTENTS

| | | |
|---|---|---|
| Prologue | | 6 |
| 1 | Old and New Wineskins | 7 |
| 2 | Covenant People | 20 |
| 3 | Institutional Roles | 45 |
| 4 | Legacy of a Mafia Parish | 60 |
| 5 | Spiritual Advisors | 78 |
| 6 | Rebuilding the Church | 91 |
| 7 | Three Tests of Fortitude | 106 |
| 8 | Parish Stories that Overlap | 114 |
| 9 | Priorities and Divine Plans | 131 |
| 10 | Religious Coping Strategies | 147 |
| 11 | The Gerousia Plan | 155 |
| 12 | Steadfast Love to God | 165 |
| 13 | The Pyx | 184 |
| Epilogue | | 191 |

\* \* \*

The characters in this story
have been modeled after those in
*The Hero with a Thousand Faces* by Joseph Campbell.
They are not unlike
the holy men and women in Catholic parishes.
The situations described are based on fictional events.

# *Prologue*

"Francis Charles Joseph Jakubowicz come forward." I use his full Christian name the Lord gave me to summon the old man out of purgatory. Leaving the grey cloud behind him, I observe a blush on his face and hesitant steps taken aback by the purest aura that surrounds his vision. He is self-conscious of the tattered clothing from the day he was murdered and waded in the river. Facing one another, I lay my hands on the top of his head, and he is suddenly made young and clothed in a bright white linen robe and adorned with a halo of stars. "I am Saint Peter. You are here to enter through the Gates of Heaven and behold your God."

Feeling overcome by the good news, the man totters; he is weak in the knees, I hold him up and lead him to one of two stately chairs within a few steps. Refreshed with a glass of water, I continue the purpose for our introduction. "We have a variety of traditions for those who enter Heaven either through the prayers of others or from their own good deeds. Yours are certainly those approaches, but there is a special ritual we have for people, who enter because a book was inspired by them. Let me show you how your life has helped others, and after I shall introduce you around and settle you into your new dwelling."

Finding him at ease I say, "call me Peter," and he says, "Frank." We sit back in our recliners with our feet up and a table of snacks and beverages on a table between us, and watch as the crystal cloud in front shows a scene from the Chicago parish of the Immaculate Conception where Frank lived only a short while ago.

# 1

# *Old and New Wineskins*

*First impressions of the retired pastor, the new pastor, and the assistant priest.*

"Remind me Father John, when is my Retreat?" I say entering the kitchen suited in my clerics, the same as theirs.

"After mine, Father Mike," my assistant is quick to respond.

The coffee maker's water is low. They must be on their second cup. Refilling it and while mine is brewing, I take out utensils to make my breakfast.

"Late night Communion call," Monsignor Luke assumes a logical reason.

"You slept through the ruckus, good."

"We had an attempted break in," John explains.

"Really? The rectory or the church? Is everyone alright?" Monsignor wants in on their information. "Did the alarms scare them? Are they on camera?"

"The church, we're good, the alarms and floodlights were effective; they were two neat-looking teens. Plus, the police response of three blaring squad cars kept them at bay while locked in the church," I fill in his answers.

"What were they thinking?"

# The Body and Blood

"Not much," John quips.

"That too, but the police said quick drug money. They told me that unreported home robberies outnumber the increase in reported ones. Home incidents mean one thing: either kids are robbing their parents or allowing their friends to. Parents file insurance claims or not, and their children go to rehab or learn the hard way. I'm making scrambled eggs. Anyone want some?"

"I'll have a small portion," Monsignor says finishing his cereal.

I look over to Father John, who nods no.

"So that's teenage crime these days. Not bad. Two unmanageable adolescents, who aren't in a gang of sorts."

"Compared with what you faced."

"What was that?" the unassimilated newcomer priest asks.

Monsignor is silent. Father John looks at me shrugging his shoulders.

"Organized crime. Are you familiar with the term?"

"You mean the Godfather movies? I watched them with a few classmates. I was told mobsters used to live around here. Their unions were controlled by your Mayor Daley. The Mafia," John says schooled.

"For sure, they are Catholic in name and criminals in deeds," the old pastor adds from firsthand knowledge.

"Some go to confession without remorse in place of a donation. They think they can buy absolution as a way to stay out of hell. Others from their psychotic or superstitious thinking rather than a guilty conscience. They have nothing to do with universal religion besides grave sinners."

"We have people like that back home. It catches up with them. The worst are antigovernment dissents, the Mafia is a step up from gangs."

"But Mafia are Catholic. If they're not checked they can be a force, an intimidating and belligerent one. They meld into a parish, receive Communion alongside the families they violate, showing us and our Eucharistic appointees as if fools for ministering to them and their families," I state a fact.

"John, your background is an Order priest. You practiced the rules of your saint and implemented his mission. You are a Diocesan priest now. Your pastor," he nods to Father Mike "and all the parish priests in this one diocese answer to the expectations of our local Bishop. You know this. I don't have to explain how vast the differences are between the needs of the people served by Order and Diocesan priests, as well as, the economies that it takes to perpetuate what those ministries involve. Before you were like a specialist compared to what you accepted to be: a general practitioner. Not to worry though, the dynamics of a neighborhood are the same anywhere in the world, it is all about the percentages of good versus evil. You will pick up what you need to know in the confessionals and focus on the bad from the pulpit. Beware though, you are a fisher of men, and hardened sinners are the proverbial sheep in wolves' clothing only subdued by angels."

"You'll catch on; however, Monsignor's right. Our Lord was an itinerant preacher for a reason and when it comes to our assignments here no one knows that better than our Bishop and his vicars. Fortunately, we like you," as pastor, I give him our reassurance.

"I always had a fondness for Order priests, a variety were my professors back in Poland. That's redemptive work to transform a college into a university, with medical and law schools that gain parochial clout. Yet, I've adapted to your Diocesan mindset of building churches and developing parish communities," John compares a vocation of many Order priests to his new role in a Diocesan ministry.

"A priest is all about a calling and being a servant to people as Christ was. My seminary education prepared me for that but on-the-job training is a step up. Your obstacles, John, are both a new culture plus a new ministry. Tough, hun?" I imagine his reality.

"Years ago, seminary training was light on subjects such as sociology and psychology. That changed in a big way. What got me through, and still does, are the five street smart and disagreeable classmates I made as friends back then," the Monsignor makes a distinction between a religious formation and the company he kept then and 45 years since.

"Not every priest is so lucky," I commend my assistant.

"Without social media impossible, but you're right. I put an ocean between me and my friends plus my family to lessen your minister shortage."

"And then there's that. What do you think, more deacons?" I am up for a conversation.

"Good men," Monsignor endorses them.

"Great men who come with families that sooner or later expect a job. No, I'm talking about priests like us, parochial trained K thru college. People say it's too myopic, too clannish," I am unimpressed with the criticisms. While serving Monsignor and me our eggs, I wait for a response.

"Not even a majority of our parishioners," the retired pastor comments.

"What. Attended all-Catholic schools?" I ask for clarification.

"That seems so."

"In Poland, public schools are like Catholic schools. They only teach about our religion," John confides in how he was raised and sips his coffee.

"Religion in America is watered down. Most preachers project their own experiences onto others and leave no room for individuals to stand out with moral courage," I look at them.

"Diocesan priests tend to focus attention on themselves through deviations in liturgy and their homilies. Church is not a place for alter egos. Those personalities God allows parishioners to crush," Monsignor says sarcastically.

"Some parishioners are self-righteous and unworthy," I flip the coin.

"Excuse me, Saint Mike," he gives a mild retort.

"I'm not being sanctimonious. I want support they don't give to pastoral work from their graces."

"Even professionals? God, we dare not give testimony to ourselves." John enjoys his food while striking a proverb.

"What are good priests?" Monsignor heeds the man who has given up his homeland and everyone to serve the faithful.

"Who builds up the Church? Who lasts?" John and I backup one another.

"In their time, the saints did. Begging the question,

what do the people of God pray for now?" Monsignor presses.

"God knows? What I know is that I have a half-a-million dollar overhead and push to show a reserve. I am trying to cut down on school expenses by qualifying for government funding, which takes another type of talent. And with two priests for four-thousand parishioners who get married, have Baptisms, First Communions, Confirmations, and eventually funerals, I wouldn't know where to start if I had spare time to be a saint," I sigh and slump back in my chair.

The assistant and retired pastor take in my complaint and momentarily break into stifled laughter, then laugh out loud. It is infectious so I hold up my glass of orange juice and say, "a toast to the saints," to which they do likewise and in unanimity we say, "Amen."

"Who is God calling? Another Fulton Sheen?" the retired pastor tosses out a name from the past.

"He was a larger than life personality, who inspired a generation of preachers and evangelists, wrote over 60 books and more in radio and TV scripts. He was certainly a man for the times, and how slow the wheels of canonization turn," I say.

"Today it's about social media chatter and the internet aka Beatified Carlos Acutis." John holds up his device.

"Mr. Purple is constantly connected," I reference my code name. "Time consuming but effective."

"Truth is religion connects with everything regardless of the latest invention. I'm not the same priest in my 80s as I was in my 20s or 50s. What stayed consistent in my ministry then, now, and tomorrow is a love for God and his people. You two will do fine. Excuse me. I'll be in the chapel to get ready for the events of the day." Monsignor says and leaves us at the table.

*The Diocesan Bishop, Reverend Lanciano.*

"Let's finish our coffee in the meeting room. I have my notes for when the Bishop calls. Here's a blank pad for you," I lead the way and we take seats on either side of an empty chair reserved for Monsignor at the conference table.

"Do you mind if I ask you a personal question?"

"Not if I can refuse to answer," he looks back confused. "Ask away."

"What do you want most for the Church?"

"Easy enough. To attract diocesan vocations."

"Me too. But as a foreigner, I have to adjust to your culture. It would have been easier if I were assigned around Pulaski Park."

"West Town and Goose Island aren't as Polish as they once were. You'll get along fine with the Italian-Americans. They're similar, love to eat, celebrate every occasion, and pray in church. Maybe Poles are not as emotional, but no nationality is," I laugh at myself and mumble, "and criminally organized." Speaking full-throated, "your focus is on the school and other duties. Whatever vocations come your way, send them to me. We share the same aims."

"In my desire to become a better man, I found Christ. The business world gave me authority I could easily misuse. Not until I entered the seminary did I straighten out the 'Lord your God' relationship, but not everyone is worthy. What conflicts do we avoid among those who aspire to join us, besides those who are unruly, disinterested in education and self-willed?

"The secret to attracting vocations is narrowing the possibilities. True, those profiles do not fit diocesan, but different religious Orders might be interested. Depends. I'll hear them out. What you and I have to do is balance our strengths and weaknesses with the resources in this parish."

"Interesting us, as prototypes?" He aspires to be a pastor someday.

"Both yes and no. We're long past our ordinations."

"Your resources are people too?"

"Plus you and me, and we can no longer manage the care of our retired pastor on top of our schedules. If we want seminarians, we have to mix with their families. If we want families to understand why their child is right for this life, we have to show them by our example. Plenty of other men and women want them, too. The priesthood is both our response to God and our service to his people through the sacraments."

"Then the focus in an early vocation is on the family first, and then the child?"

"In a way, but too few come forward and of those who do, not all are chosen."

"American marriages are a mess."

"Ergo, avoid bad ones and those who aren't willing to support their children in a career as a second choice. You're new here, to this country and this area, look around. This is an urban, low crime neighborhood for a reason and purpose. Stick to your training and your experiences. Your Bishop is your boss, and in this nation we stand for religion. People do want to win and know it takes leaders on both sides: God and Man," I take a sip of my coffee and eat a few almonds from a bowl filled in front of me, while my assistant listens regardless of the distraction. "My strengths will get me by, but there are major weaknesses that stand in the way. Time. I am overbooked with one you and no nuns. Next is my weakness to delegate. With the recent scandals, I have to weed out the indifferent. I'm confident with who I am, but perception weighs heavy on us, John. How we come across to the parishioners, how we garner their support, is not just for this house-of-worship we maintain and pray in with them: it is to save the souls who come here to worship the same Savior as ours. That's what preys on Monsignor. The parish family he leaves behind."

"Change is hard. Coming to America" he takes a deep breath. "Quick question. I promise."

"Sure." I imagine he wants a polished perspective and put my coffee cup down to pay him full attention.

"There are so many divorces, what about children from those marriages?"

"That's the hard part. To raise up intact marriages, single parents, divorced or otherwise get marginalized. It's the whole body of Christ, Father John. People get it."

"I don't. What about charismatic gifts?"

"Like I said, different Orders might be interested."

"Bias."

"Incarnation," I free associate. There is an awkward silence. "Think of it this way. You and I are fishermen. We take in what is found in our nets and make use of the entire catch, but the fish our family prefers, we bring home."

The desk phone rings. I pick up the receiver.

"Father, the Bishop's secretary called. He will be on in ten minutes," my secretary, Donna, announces.

"Please ask Monsignor to join us. He is in the chapel."

Within a few minutes, the retired pastor appears and I ask him to take the vacant seat between us.

"I've prayed for you," he says, looking at me and at John.

No one talks further and the minutes pass one by one. Even when a couple of parishioners lugging bags for the food drive come in gleefully, they catch the vibes and exit on tiptoe by the time the phone rings.

"Hello Bishop," I responded to his greeting. "Yes, I'll put you on speaker. Go ahead Bishop."

"How are you all?" the resonant voice asks.

"Good to be here, Bishop Lanciano," John replies, filling in the hesitation.

"Monsignor Luke, are you there?" the Bishop asks.

"I'm here Greg and rather not be in this spot."

"I understand. No one relishes this kind of a conversation. It is necessary though. We all want to do this the right way. Father Leonardi, would you go first."

"Thank you, Bishop. I have three points to make. I'll stop after each one." I refer to my notepad. "First, let me say Bishop, that I am grateful for my assistant; however, we remain two men in a parish with four-thousand parishioners to answer for. Monsignor remains an asset. But Church regulations dictate, we cannot employ a health aide to work in the rectory as a staff member," I pause.

"Agreed. Let me ask you specifically. What are those tasks?" We hear the Bishop rustle some papers.

"On a monthly basis, there are trips to and from four doctors and a weekly physical therapy appointment, along with supervision of his daily medications. Two parish men have volunteered for this duty. When neither can make it, these consultations fall on Father John. This happens often."

"Um. Monsignor Luke, you're a big man. Your bevy of ladies can't do this work for you," the Bishop chides him, and we stifle a laugh. "Silent? Okay Father, your next point."

"The stairs. Our bedrooms are on the second floor reached by too narrow a staircase for a chair lift. I am out of my mind, if God forbid. I dare not say it."

"This is a problem, Luke. You can't let your health issues rest entirely on these priests. I want you to seriously consider their position in the community if you were to lose your balance and fall," the Bishop confronts the main point, but Monsignor gives no defense.

"Finally, there are personal hygiene routines Father John and I take turns helping Monsignor but mishaps occur. We are kind and capable, Bishop. Our challenge is the time it takes to attend to our brother in between managing a parish of four thousand souls that includes a school."

"I thank you for holding your own financially and giving the diocese a surplus, Father Leonardi. I have to hear from you Luke. We are one in our commitment to you."

"I'll go," he is expressionless.

"No push back? Where's my sparring partner? That is all you have to say, 'I'll go.' You aren't more in need of care than just old," the Bishop insists, as if with a slap on the back.

"What can I say, it's all true. And then, there is the other side. God wants me here. The people of this parish want me here."

"Yes, they do," the Bishop's tone is appreciative. "You worked miracles, and you will always be loved by them. You are a treasure of the Church, a true servant of Christ, and a brother apostle, one with us. You're getting ready, Luke. It didn't happen like you or your people wanted it to happen. We are trying to help you own that. They have a shepherd who loves them too, wouldn't you say?" The Bishop seeks closure.

"He's young."

"I'm 42!" I balk.

"He has a temper," Monsignor tries to spur me on.

"He's a human being," the Bishop referee's. "He's middle aged, graduate level, with almost twenty years of pastoral experience. He's hardly young."

"He doesn't know seventy and eighty year olds. He'll underestimate them."

"He'll learn."

"The hard way," Monsignor replies, assuming a valid concern.

"Wait. I'm neither naïve nor inexperienced with old people. I have a family. I protest."

"A parish family is different and each member is unique.

These old people are subtle, affluent, and some have real issues and others real talents," Monsignor knows.

"Luke, you can't pour new wine into old wineskins. We have already trusted him with the keys. God's plan is a learning curve that we have mastered many times over through grace in his Word and Spirit."

"So be it. I said my piece. He will learn from experience and God will be with him."

"Well said. Peace be with you" the Bishop seals the decision.

"And also with you," the three of us respond.

"In the words of Our Lord, Jesus Christ, 'Whoever serves me must follow me, and where I am, there also will my servant be. The Father will honor whoever serves me.' God bless you and your parishioners, brethren," the Bishop signs off.

"Thank you, Bishop Lanciano," as pastor, I reply respectfully to end the conversation.

# 2

# *Covenant People*

*While Monsignor prays in the quiet of the Church, two parishioners overhear him.*

The back of the church is dark in contrast to the well-lit altar, but many candles illuminate the statue of St. Anthony, where I pray for his grace. Midday I expect to be alone, so I look to identify the slow shuffle of a person moving down the front aisle. The man I remember, who walked briskly around the track at our local park, is no longer to be found. When Monsignor Luke reaches the steps of the sanctuary, instead of proceeding, he stands with arms outstretched as if to mirror the image of Christ crucified above the altar. I think about leaving but suddenly hear him speak.

"Father, I want to stay with my people."

I am drawn in. First, by utter silence broken by a loud voice, and then, by the sad petition.

"Heavenly Host, have I not loved them with all my heart? Have I not shepherded them with all my strength as your Son?" The words break his lament. Approaching his 90s, he struggles to kneel and in doing so remains erect like the towering steeple atop the parish church he and his loyal followers helped to build.

"Christ, have I not adored your house with prayer and celebration enough to prove my love for them? Have I not made your people mine for the glory of the Almighty? I have given you everything," he says with a passion as deep as his seeming defeat.

I stay silent with bated breath. The Monsignor prays more and then rises to his feet. Labored in his walk to the back, the sacristan comes out of the sacristy, having been there unbeknownst to us. She embraces him and says something uplifting. A foot taller than her, he pats her head like a young child. About to leave, he turns towards the altar, bows and makes the sign of the cross.

"Please, come and visit with me, whomever you are praying to Our Lord."

He senses someone and without hesitation, I come forward to greet him with a hug. We are as father and daughter with a bond of priest and parishioner for thirty years. "Are you really leaving Monsignor?"

"Tomorrow, Laurel."

"We are all very sad, you know? We will visit you often, I promise."

"In the beginning," he leaves off and lifts my face with tearful eyes smiling back at him.

"You're right, but you will be in my thoughts much more often. It is an odd feeling to grow old."

"And forgetful, and off balance," he says, annoyed with the facts that force him to retreat from his parish home. His candor restores our normal dispositions.

"He's young," I blurt out.

"So was Christ," he reminds me.

"He won't care about us old folk."

"He will. I reassure you. Do you want to know why?"

"There are obvious reasons but yes, why?"

"Because I am in a sacred covenant with God and entrusting you, and the sacristan, and others to help him help you."

I would smile at the cliché except Monsignor expresses the idea as if for the first time. I am in awe of his courage.

"You have a soul I am very invested in. I know how daring you can be. You never shy away from a tough question and for some reason—a grace from God—people answer you," he says amused. "No doubt, it comes from your schooling as a psychologist, a gift and talent God has given you. I know what you were praying for though. You were asking St. Anthony to intercede on what happened to your stepfather, weren't you?"

Reflexively, my head bends in humility.

"Frank went missing on my watch. You are not alone in seeking God's truth," he turns his head away to hide the reflection of his disappointment in so many public prayers from the community unanswered. "I asked several of your friends to pray for one another. They have struggles also, but some sinners never change. We tend to be idealistic. I worry about that."

It is on the hour and the bells of the church begin to ring one by one.

"I care about people's mental health. Thoughts can be hard to tame. I admit I am a better listener than a doer sometimes," he gives me a quizzical smirk. "I'll work on my feelings about Frank in confession."

"Good girl," and in his natural manner he pats me on the head, as well. "Pray for me?"

If I answer, he will leave. Fighting my emotions, I say, "Yes, Father. Always."

There will be a void from his decades of emotional support. The new pastor does not know my story which is complicated and involves a missing person. Yet, if Monsignor sees me capable of renewing our type of relationship with his successor in the same spiritual light, I accept his insight.

---

*Father John takes charge of Monsignor's moving day.*

From the terrace off my bedroom in the rectory, I pray the Divine Office for priests and glance up at times to watch as parishioners park their cars and walk up to the church for the 9 o'clock Mass. Uncharacteristically, they are stopping to gather in the courtyard in small groups and pairs to talk. As if through osmosis, whether in America or in my native home of Poland, Catholics know when something major happens, such as one of their priest's relocating. In Monsignor's instance, it is far from a reassignment to another parish. Different from their wishes, but beyond the control of our staff to manage his health care, they will understand that only the Bishop could have made the decision to move him to the diocese's retirement home. With Monsignor Luke absent in his seat at Mass among the congregation this morning, this crowd might guess or have heard indirectly that his departure is today.

Finished with my prayers, I go to his room and hurry to pack last minute possessions left in his suite. Alexa announces from the living room at volume 10, "Your thirty-minute timer is up," she repeats.

"Alexa, stop," my voice is raised.

"Good idea to have her speed us along," Alex Moretti, my moving helper and towering ex-fireman from the parish, says to support me.

"We're down to 25-minutes before the 9 is out," I respond from Monsignor's bathroom as I swoop my hand from one end of the medicine cabinet shelf to the other and empty the sundries into a small box. Repeating the action three times, I close the door as I found it. "Everything is out of this room."

"Come in here and tell me which paintings to pack."

The two of us stand side-by-side, sweaty and tense, with scattered boxes half-filled, filled, and empty. We could be mistaken for moving men or for thieves.

"Look, this painting." Alex points decisively to Rembrandt's Prodigal Son.

"Definitely. We spent hours talking about it. Let's be careful," I help him pack the large framed artwork in bubble wrap.

"Your twenty-minute timer is up."

"Alexa, stop," and then to Alex, "Hand me that empty box."

With it, I scoop up a pile of reading material, papers, and stationary left on a coffee table. "He wrote his correspondence sitting in front of the TV. He'll want these."

"Here," Alex tosses me a box of chocolates.

"Can't forget that. The pastor brought him this

yesterday. Still unopened, I guess it didn't do much to ease the good-bye."

"Monsignor wanted to die here as much as his friends wanted him to. God's plan?" he points to a small icon image of the Crucifixion on the wall.

I nod "yes," adding a hand swipe with a double meaning that the icon be packed.

"He'll be missed for sure. Let's get him where he should be. What about all these?" He points to a pile of small gift wrapped items in a desk drawer he has opened.

"He would bring those rosaries on sick calls. Take them. He can give them to his visitors," I scan the living room and toss a pair of slippers in one more box. "That looks like it. Off to the van."

"Roger that."

"Is that an American idiom?" I have turned into a constant language learner. Draping a windbreaker on top of a large box that Alex is about to carry out the door, I follow him down the staircase with another.

"Roger that is a military code to copy what someone says in your action. You must have a similar expression?"

"Yesh," I say in an exaggerated accent trying to lessen the mood.

"Your fifteen-minute timer is up," Alexa announces.

"Alexa, stop," we yell lightheartedly, and with two more trips up and down, we are finished under schedule and cancel the timer.

Once outside, Gene Lustig, a parishioner and owner of the packed van, and Marco, a young and strong borrowed employee of the gardener, takeover. Already, they have Monsignor buckled in the back seat ready to relocate him to his new residence and suite. I watch them drive away with the beloved priest.

My morning is on a tight schedule. I am the celebrant at the 9:45 funeral Mass. As I head into the church to prepare, the 9 is finishing with attendees reciting their final prayers. At an opposite doorway, I see Alex with the bright sunlight behind him step forward and give an obvious prearranged signal to the pastor and says softly, "it is finished." Several parishioners' heads turn. The choice of words is astonishing. The penultimate last words of Christ. There is no doubt that a man, a pastor, of great spiritual distinction has physically left.

---

*After the 9, the women have breakfast at the diner.*

Groups of us linger in the front of the church talking about Monsignor, but are curtailed by the gathering of family and friends who watch the pallbearers carry the casket of their loved one slowly processing inside for a funeral Mass.

Ava says to Sophie, "let's tell the others to meet us at the diner."

"They left already, and said that they would wait for us to eat," and likewise, the women depart.

When the others arrive ahead of them, the diner is packed with locals and workers taking their breakfast break on a late shift. Pretty much in the center of the room, five of the alt-group are seated. Alternative because, each has an account as to why she is childless.

One of the seven women seated now, Laurel, asks the others, "What do you think will happen to him?"

"Ah, it's so sad. I heard Monsignor rang the doorbell of Marie Grange's house, thinking it was the rectory. He really ought to be in a protected environment," Rosa informs them.

"Marie called to tell me what happened," Claire reinforces the account.

"I heard the priests were mostly worried Monsignor would fall down the stairs from his bedroom. The staircase is too narrow to install a lift," Deanna says following up with, "if you know that could happen, like they do, and fail to act, the blame would be on them for not acting."

"They would be guilty," Mia is quick to condemn.

"Not necessarily, their defense is the consent of Monsignor plus diocesan regulations, not house rules that forbid an aide to work in the rectory which seemed religious in origin to me, but reasons of liability are as meaningful. A fall would just be an accident," Laurel admits to their logic but not to anyone's fault.

"Here they are," Rosa spots the two ladies talking with the hostess and waves to Ava and Sophie, who lose no time in taking their empty seats.

"The crowd got big in front of the church. It's chilly out there," Sophie takes a seat, straightening her clothes and hooking her handbag on a fashion accessory that she attaches to the table.

"The funeral was for Madeline Jaffoni. Remember her? She was big in the Rosarians, then she moved with her son out to the island after her husband died. Good person, Madeline.

Always a big help for Sister Theresa when she would do the raffles," Ava eulogizes.

"Good Morning, my beautiful ladies. How is everyone this morning?" The waiter has his pad and pencil ready along with his pleasant disposition.

"Good Morning, Hugo," the women reply in unanimity and small talk, followed by his question. "Same all around?"

Five are heard in her response, "Same." "Me, too." "Yes." "Same." "I'll have the same." "I would like the parfait yogurt, today," Rosa changes it up. "Mm's" are heard and without more said, the last is up. "The usual. I don't really care what I eat this morning," Deanna seems to prefer a morale booster more than breakfast.

"Ah, what's the matter Deanna? Everything okay?" Rosa is first to solve a problem.

"No. Everything is good," she gives a mixed message. "It's just. Well, I heard a few parishioners blame Father John for objecting to take care of Monsignor. They're both such good priests, but Father John's job isn't that. Not at this level and duration," she defends him.

Two waiters go around the table filling their coffee cups asking each to choose "decaf or regular?"

"I get that. My mom is a full time responsibility." Ava agrees, and then is interrupted by Sophie.

"At a hundred and one and with an aide."

"Still, Monsignor is like a father to me, and he's my confessor. I wanted him to stay. I have to make special plans to visit him."

"Me too. I've gone to Monsignor for confession as long as you," Claire seconds.

"We have to start all over with a new confessor. That's the real problem," Sophie underscores.

"Good thing he heard mine a few days ago," Rosa's eyes are focused on her sumptuous parfait.

"Don't we sound like a bevy of nuns, and each of us schooled by them. So, tell me Sisters, who here does not confess to Monsignor?" Laurel asks, and no one raises her hand. "Interesting. Well, I can only speak for myself, but with him twenty-miles away at a retirement home, I have no intention of disturbing his peace-of-mind, but I do need another Spiritual Director."

"He might refuse," Sophie quips.

"Who? The next victim, I mean priest?" Claire adds more humor.

"Monsignor would never refuse to hear my confession. A priest can't unless the person refuses to reform or isn't sorry. What would be the point of it?" Ava is unamused and confident of her influence.

"Ava, he's old and has health issues," Deanna appeals to her reasoning.

"He requires a lot of time and attention, going back and forth to doctors. Monsignor and my husband are both tall men. When Paul fell last week, I had to call the fire department to pick him up. We were blessed it was nothing more serious," says Rosa.

"My dad was a lot of work a few years before he died,"

Mia's comment is a vivid reminder to us.

"We have neighbors who are aides for my mom. At some point, you cannot leave an old person Home Alone. Um, a reverse movie, like Benjamin Button," Laurel thinks of movie options to cope.

"She's right. Parish outreach groups and neighbors are helpful, but not everyone is capable of fitting all the pieces together," Mia says.

"Like what?" two women say simultaneously.

"We could use a more expansive ministry organized within the parish. A team who knows about aides, insurance, health care equipment, legal consultants, plus medical professionals," Sophie makes a pitch. "Some of us have no families left, and despite our finances and the wherewithal to live independently, we all need oversight. All the pieces are in the parish community ready to be organized.

"Well, Monsignor or an older priest might have considered your ideas, but we have a young pastor and assistant. We're seniors living alone in our houses, our condos that young families, who might be Catholics, want and priests who would see things more their way than ours," Laurel sums up.

"Ah! Speaking of our properties, Marsy Berger, the Realtor, is a few tables away with what looks like buyers. I get a mailing from her more regularly than from my sister," Deanna's tone is sarcastic.

"Well, we live in a desirable neighborhood. Compact enough where everyone can know everyone. There are six houses of worship and five elementary schools in a four-mile square area. As much as we want to grow old and die here, like we wanted for Monsignor, young families with children pray to move in," Claire says.

"No one wants change, especially him and us. To relocate our confessor of 30 years, who knows us like a book, this is terrible. Until I make up my mind, I'm going to confess to whomever, when- and where- ever it is convenient for me. Right now, I wonder if the pastor will take over Monsignor's Sunday 8AM Mass. His old-timers go to that one," Mia shifts the spotlight.

"That would be one way to show he cares. However," Laurel stresses her words in a way to set up a note of humor. "If the pastor wants to cultivate us seniors, he ought to be more purposeful than forming an I.C. Friends group. Those mid-week gatherings after Mass were awkward for the women and the men."

A few of us salute the reference but all laugh heartily.

"I went once, that was enough. Didn't you get the picture?" Claire gives a silly smirk at the obvious with a wakeup slap down of her hand on the table.

Their banter is whimsical, with each overlapping.

"Did you see how many donuts Ralph Aliano ate? Marge Lorenzo tucked a couple in her handbag."

"Then, the deli delivered a huge bag of bagels and cream cheese for our diets."

"Mike and Richie kept coming in and out of the room, as if they were afraid to stand in one spot too long. Fear of engagement."

"Wishful Thinking."

"On whose part?"

"I don't know? I think a couple women: Arlene Marino and Peggy Flynn looked fetching dressed up for the morning socials?"

"Those two old schoolers. Every day is dress up Sunday with a hat."

"Father has the wrong group. I don't know what he had in mind, but it wasn't in anyone else's mind."

"Was it an attempt at matchmaking? Half of us are taking care of our aged parents, and the other half haven't been on a date in thirty- forty- years."

"Speak for yourself, missy," Rosa chimes in.

"He means well I guess? Personally, I think he is using projection for an idea he wants himself, to be married," Laurel applies a defense mechanism and slows the conversation down.

"I'm not going to feel sorry for him," Sophie is definite.

"Don't worry. The I.C. Friends group will end pretty soon when none of you make a move. Haven't you noticed the married men and women were the first to stop going?" Deanna reassesses.

"Stop, Stop," Ava says with a snicker. "Either we think we are undesirable or so out-of-date we've forgotten what it was like to be romantic. This is goofy, and our food is getting cold."

"Not mine. I'm eating a parfait," Rosa laughs at herself.

"And another thing," Mia speaks up. "The Pastor should stop thinking we are looking to catch him in a scandal. We all support his right to seek vocations one-hundred percent."

"Interesting," Deanna rolls her eyes smiling. "You don't want to keep one for yourself?

"There are other fish," our waiter Hugo overhears the conversation and jests as he passes the table onto the next.

"You're a flirt," Ava raises her voice loud enough to tease him back.

"Mia is right though," our heads turn to Sophie for clarification. "Aside from the sarcasm, all any of us want, after working our whole lives, is to share more time with friends with our families fading, to enjoy our home life and our spiritual interests leisurely. None of us want to get in the way of anyone, least of all their religious process." No one interrupts. "Remember what Monsignor used to say. We have to help the parish priests help us, and to pray for one another. He always gave us good advice and never misled us."

"Okay. Let's think of that. How is each of us involved in the church?" Claire challenges. "Lector, Eucharistic minister, visits to the homebound, Rosarians, Third-Order Franciscans, our commitment to religious education, and then in our families, caring for a loved one. Include the time you spend on maintaining your home, doing chores, sharing quality time with friends, like now. I would say that it fills my calendars. You ladies?"

"I'm thoroughly occupied," Deanna, who is married, answers first.

"When I have a sitter for my mom, I go to Mass and do Communion calls, attend a wake when one happens, help out in the rectory. In my down time, I do chores and watch a movie, some news. Maybe, I could give the church a few more hours during the week, but doing what?" Ava asks for ideas.

"Forgive me if I sound speechy," Laurel says. "We are not here to be patronized for our individuality. In our lifetime, our religion came first. What we learned at home or were taught in school, at some point the lessons took hold in what we said and did. Whether religion meant to attend Sunday Mass, to tithe our income to our parish or school, or how we went about marrying and desiring to bring children into the world, our Catholic faith became more than a pick and choose religion to us. It is our nature. If you don't believe me, why are we doing all this churchy stuff? Our priests chose us for our willingness," she pauses.

"I don't trust them," Mia says.

"And there's the rub," Ava snaps.

"Why not?" Rosa asserts. She is friends with her the longest.

"If you don't give them money, like us up front, they take it one way or another in a Last Will or donations, and they use it however they want."

"Do you want the safe haven of the Church or not? Without the companionship of us and all of us in the parish, do you really believe you would have thrived as you and your brother have?" Claire demands a response.

"Maybe."

"Really? Your parents brought you to this neighborhood over 50 years ago. What were you 20 years old? You grew up in the house they left you, you and your brother remained single, childless, and retired from your jobs with that bio. Now, you are both old, without an extended family, and you believe you accomplished all that alone? Wait, don't answer," she holds up her index finger teaching her a lesson. "You are our family as much as you are to one another, unless you have no faith in our love." Claire is hardly ever upset and hurt, but she is now.

Two of the women's cell phones ring and they answer.

"No,"

"Oh my God. That's horrible."

Deanna and Rosa underscore parts of their tense conversations with their callers, taking turns to relay the news of how the van that had brought Monsignor to his retirement home, upon its return to the parish, was in an accident. The young man died on the scene.

"God rest his soul. Thank God Monsignor wasn't in the van," Rosa says.

The response is a collective sound of "Amen."

"The young man, I don't think any of us knew him, Marco?"

"I do," Deanna answers. "The gardener brings him along when he comes to my house, a strong man, early twenties, polite, good worker, respectful to his boss. I only had a few words with him. I remember he said that he had one year left of college before making any big decisions with his life."

"His parents will be devastated," Claire surmises. "What happened to Gene? How did the accident happen?"

"Go ahead," Rosa says to Deanna as they talk over one another.

"You know where that turn is at the backend of the

Park? How you have to concentrate more on following the curve than on the road beneath," the women acknowledge they do. "Apparently, there was a large pothole, and the tire on the passenger side got trapped in it and the van rolled over. Marco, they say, never regained consciousness and died on the scene. Such a waste of a life."

"Terrible for Gene Lustig, too. He was starting to fit into the parish. I don't know him well, bits and pieces of his background. Poor guy," Laurel says empathically.

"This will be a lot for everyone to overcome," Ava says.

"Rosa. Ava. Laurel. Your take-home orders are at the counter. Ladies, I have your check," Hugo looks around at whose turn it is to pay. Our mood has changed completely.

---

*Father Mike administers the sacrament of the Anointing of the Sick formerly called Extreme Unction or Last Rites.*

Instead of reading my Midday Office, I listen to it on my IPhone en route to give Gene Last Rites at the hospital. I find him in an Emergency Room bed hooked up with various monitoring devices, lucid if a little sedated.

"Mike, Father Leonardi," he corrects himself. "He's dead. My God, the kid died. I was driving."

The man, over twenty years my senior, a retired case manager, feels self-loathing of the type he has counseled others against. Weeping uncontrollably and afraid he will add to his complications, I hold his head to my shoulder.

"How am I going to live with myself? His parents must be heartbroken. He was twenty-two years old. His life is gone."

Gene rattles off his most pressing pain. I seek to dispel it, stepping away.

"The community, the parish family of Immaculate Conception, we are going to help you heal. I will personally comfort the parents. From what I heard about Marco, his soul is set for heaven. You have to attend to yours."

"Ough! My side. I must have been hurt in the accident," Gene is distracted more by his physical pain than his distraught emotions.

"The ER doctor told me he scheduled an x-ray for your side. If nothing is broken, you can leave in a few hours. Gene, I cannot wait for that. I have confessions at noon."

"I thought I was dead. I wasn't driving fast. The front tire fell into a hole and the van toppled over. The kid hit his head, but something else happened. I can't remember. He had blood across his stomach."

"He was wearing a belt rake that turned inward and pierced an artery. He bled out in minutes. There was nothing anyone could have done for him."

"God help me. Please, God. He died."

"Do you want me to hear your confession?" after a lapse of twenty-some years, it would be his second one.

"Please."

Taking out my stole, kissing it, and placing the purple cloth over my neck, I ask him to start.

"Bless me Father for I have sinned. I know I told you most of what happened in my marriage. I couldn't bring myself to tell you everything along with the annulment, but now

Marco. There's a parallel."

He hesitates. I say, "Go ahead. God loves you."

"I made myself sound like my wife and I worked equally to have a child. We started out, you know 'begotten not made.' Not so easy. I had medical complications, spermatozoa. I went along, took meds for almost a year and then got impatient, dwelt on what was wrong with me, hated myself, did drugs, got into orgies. My doc and I kept my VD to ourselves. My wife never knew, even after I divorced her. Don't you see, I took Marco away from his parents just as I took the child away in my marriage. I made my wife infertile. Father, she remarried still wanting a family. How does God forgive that?"

Looking back stoically, he becomes tearful, and I allow him to feel contrite.

"Please, help me to forgive myself."

There is no purpose to question him further. Deathbed confessions and most of the dying have horrific sins to leave behind on their journey to the afterlife. Guilt over the taking or prevention of life is common in dissolved marriages or abandoned relationships. Apparently, a guilty conscience has allowed Gene to rationalize the complications of his divorce long enough. For his sake, I recognize the blessing God offers him to do penance and will help him amend his past life.

"The death of Marco was an accident, but the secret you kept from your wife will be harder for you to forgive yourself. Our Blessed Virgin Mother suffered greatly in sharing with us the kind of life she held within her, the Incarnate Word of God who became man to redeem our sins. If you respect women in some measure to her, you can atone for your sins," he acknowledges my rebuke with a bowed head.

"I can. I have faith that I can," penitently, he recites an Act of Contrition.

"I came here not knowing what condition I would find you in and prepared to administer Last Rites. I have done half of that in hearing your confession, and have the Holy Oil and Eucharist with me to conclude this sacrament."

"Please, Father."

After reciting The Lord's Prayer together, I open the bottle of holy oil and pour some on my thumb to trace the sign of the cross on his forehead reciting the blessing, "Through this holy anointing may the Lord in his love and mercy help you with the grace of the Holy Spirit. May the Lord who frees you from sin save you and raise you up." Then, removing the pyx from the sick call case, I take the host between my fingers and raise the Eucharist to him saying, "This is the Lamb of God who takes away the sins of the world. Happy are those who are called to his supper."

"Lord, I am not worthy to receive you, but only say the word and I shall be healed," he responds and receives the host as I place it on his tongue in submission. Truly, I believe Mr. Lustig will be a changed man. A year later, he becomes one of our parish Eucharistic Ministers.

---

*He administers the Sacrament of Reconciliation, also called Penance or Confession.*

By the time I drive home, there are fifteen minutes to prepare for noon confessions. Rather than stop in my room, I go straight to the sacristy, hang up my jacket, kiss and place another purple stole around my neck, turn the lights to dim in the main church and set the recorder to play a Benedictine

Gregorian tape. Going to the sanctuary, I sit in my chair and take the spare time to collect my thoughts for the two hours ahead of me. "My God, your people carry such heavy crosses. Inspire me with your words to lift their burdens and heal their broken spirits, especially for the repose of Marco and for the redemption of Gene." Once taken up in prayer, soothed by the harmony of the sound of one voice in many, my mind recuperates from a day seemingly spent.

"Father, Father Leonardi," a child whispers loudly from the steps to the altar. "Are you hearing confession, Father?"

Out of my reverie, the child, her mother and I walk to the confessional booths, where I hear the venial sins of an innocent girl so welcomed at this moment. Once finished, I wait for the next penitent to arrive. The light footsteps of a person approaching readies me. A familiar noise of someone sitting is heard on the other side of the partition. Simultaneously, the red glow of the lightbulb above the door frame in my booth goes on. I slide open the panel and through the screen, the person is cued.

"Bless me Father for I have sinned. It has been about a month since my last confession," a woman's voice is heard.

"Father, this is Laurel. Can you slide the screen open please?"

Even in her whispered tone, I recognize her voice. She is one of my lectors; otherwise, I might not agree to the request. I keep my face in profile.

"Father, Monsignor Luke has always heard my confessions."

She is one of his loyal followers who I want to cultivate.

"You know me through my ministries and also my mom. I am privileged to be taking care of her. She was also a Eucharistic Minister and religious instructor for 15 years."

Immediately, I imagine a purpose to this third party in the confessional with us.

"My sin has to do with our ministries and a problem I have with us carrying them out."

Her voice quivers, and as she composes herself, I remain still. Confession is often an emotional sacrament.

"You don't know our story. I would have no reason to bring it up, it happened 25 years ago, except for everything that has been going on. My mother's husband, Frank, my stepfather, became a missing person in his 80s. Life moves fast when people are as committed to the duties of work as my mom and I were. We kept pace and let the police do their work."

She stops. I ask what seems an obvious question. "Was he ever found?"

"No. Monsignor would announce the circumstances regarding Frank after Sunday Masses for a month. He was the Treasurer of the Holy Name Society and married in this church. Our business friends took charge and put his picture and reward information on page three of the Beacon for a year. No one ever came forward. Frank was finally declared deceased five years later. Even then, it is hard to adjust without knowing the truth," she pauses and discloses. "Father, this past week we received a Christmas card addressed to Mrs. Frank Jakubowicz and daughter from a person whose name belongs to a mobster who used to live in the neighborhood. My mom recognized it right away and let slip that he wanted her business and to avoid ever talking about him. Could a person be so bold? If it is him who killed my stepfather, what does he want this time?"

"What is your sin, Laurel?" This is not my first murder mystery. Confession is a brief format and like most penitents she assumes I can make all the connections she leaves out. She has no course of action. I am unconvinced at the moment.

"Since this person lived in the neighborhood at the time when Frank went missing, and my mom was a Eucharistic Minister and religion teacher, and I was a lector, we might have given the murderer of Frank Holy Communion, religious instructions to his children, and read the Word of God from the pulpit to him. I can't believe our faith asks us to forgive like that?"

The darkness of the booth matches my feeling. "Again, Laurel, what is your sin?"

"I'm overwhelmed. Is murder and forgiveness of it that easy? Confess it to a priest, receive Holy Communion, listen to and be instructed on the Word of God from the victims without their knowledge. No wonder he wants more, if taking from us is that easy."

"Laurel, you and your mother accepted an order of commission to act as ministers. Besides, confession is not fiction. You don't have facts. The way you present it is real to you, but not to me. This happened a long time ago. In what way do you feel Frank's disappearance is unresolved for you?" I beg the question to which if she answers I can help her formulate her thoughts into a sin. I am uncomfortable less with the crime and more with the theological implications.

"A murder was committed and dismissed as insignificant. Frank was a righteous man with three children plus me, seven grandchildren, and back then two great-grandchildren. True our parish community helped us through the ordeal, but what does that mean if one of them killed him and others covered it up. I imagine everybody thought the mob but no one dared to say so and now this Christmas card. In the name of God, why were my mother and me expected to serve this parishioner by offering him the Eucharist? We were asked by the religious to serve. We never thought to volunteer for these ministries."

"You and your mom were in real estate. Isn't it more likely that this person was someone you did business with years ago and thought of you with a Christmas card? I assume you pursued your case with the legal authorities fully," I want her to consider a different possibility, not to deter her belief, but to confess to her course of action one way or the other.

"Father, I promise you my motive is purely righteousness for a good and gentle man missing and whom most people in this parish suspect was murdered. Both my mother's and my cars were stolen within the same month. The murderer is pursuing me, not the other way around. Before now, we never received a card from this notorious person. If I am reacting to feelings, they are of helplessness. That is my sin."

"If you fear for your life, the police can protect you. For now, you received a Christmas card and let your imagination build a case around it. The case is unresolved and closure is missing. I will pray for the Holy Spirit to enlighten you, and that God the Son with his mighty archangels continue to watch over you and your mother as your stepfather would want," she gives no rebuttal. I proceed with absolution and penance. "For your sins say three Our Fathers," and then prays, "God the Father of mercies, through the death and resurrection of his Son has reconciled the world to himself and sent the Holy Spirit among us for the forgiveness of sins; through the ministry of the Church may God give you pardon and peace, and I absolve you from your sins. In the name of the Father, and of the Son, and of the Holy Spirit. Amen."

"Thank you, Father. May I ask one last question?"

I allow her.

"In the absence of Monsignor would you be my Spiritual Director?"

Forgive me Heavenly Father, I ask her to wait.

# 3

# *Institutional Roles*

*Father Mike is guided by his Spiritual Director, Father Mark.*

A much older man than I, my Spiritual Director relationship with Father Mark is a standing appointment every other Thursday evening at Holy Name Cathedral, a twenty-minute walk. A strict observant of tradition, he creates our time together as a systematic activity which over the years helps me to connect my past to the present. In turn, I am a Spiritual Director to others and, like him, take this role seriously. We have no choice but to limit the people we counsel given the religious purpose we serve and the schedules we keep.

My meeting with Father Mark is for an hour and either starts or ends with my confession and then involves a topic of my pastoral concerns. For the past month, I have used the same outline which we have made much progress on.

Attracting and Directing Vocations

Through Parishioners and Parish Groups

I. Which People Attract and How They Direct Vocations

• Parents: family masses, grace before meals, night prayers, church socials.

• K-12 teachers: parochial and home school students in their religious curriculum, plus altar servers, lectors, student government leaders.

- Religious educators: sacramental instruction for Catholic public school students.

- Priests and Deacons: homilies, organizations, societies, priest's meetings open to all parishioners.

## II. Which Parish Groups Attract and How They Direct Vocations

- Grandparents, elders: parish societies, special events.

- Peers: diocesan events, parish ministries, teen societies.

- Nine o'clock Mass attendees: work ethic carryover, disciplined, grateful, sociable with tested religious values.

- Parish groups: small groups, large societies with religious values tied to pastoral corporal and spiritual works.

- Outliers: civics, businesses, professionals as sponsors and mentors, connect their interests to religious charism.

## III. Potential Vocations: Nature/Nurture

- Called by: God through examples of priests, family, parishioners, Catholic media representatives, and the like.

- Nurtured by: parents, close family, and child's nature.

- Driven by: modern culture, religious movement, traditions, theology.

---

*Vesting and Easter Vigil entrance prayers.*

As pastor, I am principal the celebrant for the Easter Vigil, the high point of the Triduum and the end of Lent. The Mass that marks the culmination of the passion, death, and

# The Body and Blood

resurrection of Jesus Christ. Without this celebration and my entire faith in it, my priesthood would be other than Catholic.

We are taught to take the people of God as they are with our mutual commitment to improve. Approximately, half of the 1.3 billion Catholics in the world attend Mass once a month. Catholics who remain dormant in the practice of their faith for extended periods are called the lapsed. Do I wish that would change? Of course, I want a full house, a royal flush, every Sunday. Until those days come, I work with the chosen people God has sent to me.

On the topic of vocations, the young children who are altar servers are the most promising to mold into future religious or into lay adults dedicated to the faith. Whether their spiritual development leads them to the priesthood, married or single life, the fortitude to remain Catholic often starts from this positive experience. Offering Mass in their presence with eyes of faith that adults are sometimes too preoccupied to imagine anymore, my self-doubts that the spirit calls us to serve for a holy purpose disappear.

Our sacristy is a small room, 15 x 30 feet and too small to accommodate tonight's lectors, Matt and Laurel, and two extra Eucharistic Ministers, who have taken their seats in the front pew of the congregation of the thousand-person capacity gathered. In the still overcrowded room where I vest, three altar servers and two deacons remain. The deacons, neighborhood men, are off to the side chatting about last week's Easter gifts sold in the vestibule by our visiting vendor from Bethlehem. Our servers are siblings, two brothers and their sister from our school. I use this preparation time to go through the steps of vesting as trained and for my altar servers' observation in the hope that one or both of them will do the same someday.

Around the parish, I make it a practice to wear my

clerical clothing. You know that priest outfit of a black shirt with black pants, or the black pants with the black shirt and most noticeable our starched white collar, a public symbol of Roman identification. In my down time, I prefer casual wear in tans with blues or greens. Apart from either modest attire tonight, I am comfortable in liturgical vestments that represent the glory of our Paschal celebration of the Lord's Last Supper and his triumphant resurrection after death.

To start, I wash my hands in the sacrarium we use to clean the sacred elements and vessels and then close the lid over the sink so as not to misuse it. I say the prescribed prayer loud enough for the altar servers to hear, "Give virtue to my hands, O Lord, that being cleansed from all stains I might serve you with purity of mind and body."

From my vestment closet, I remove the amice, a white linen shawl, place it around my shoulders and lace the strings crisscrossing my chest behind my waist and to the front again and then tie a knot saying, "Place upon me, O Lord, the helmet of salvation, that I may overcome the assaults of the devil." Like the altar servers, I wear an Alb tied with a cincture. Pulling over my head the long white Alb – mine is hemmed in a wide decorative lace – it falls to the bottom of my trousers. As I tie the cincture, a rope, around my waist I pray, "Make me clean, O Lord, and cleanse my heart; that being made white in the Blood of the Lamb I may deserve an eternal reward. Gird me, O Lord, with the cincture of purity, and quench in my heart the fire of concupiscence, that the virtue of continence and chastity may abide in me."

The stole for tonight is a luxurious novelty fabric embroidered with a gold filament design. I kiss the center of its neck and place it over mine saying, "Lord, restore the stole of immortality, which I lost through the collusion of our first parents, and, unworthy as I am to approach Thy sacred mysteries, may I yet gain eternal joy."

My chasuble is heavy and ornate. A thick white velvet vestment edged in a gold lamé scrolled embroidery, covered in an elaborate vine and floral pattern over the front and on the back an outlined image of the body of Christ with arms outstretched to us in a beaded needlepoint of muted colors. "O Lord, who has said, 'My yoke is sweet and My burden light,' grant that I may so carry it as to merit Thy grace."

Fully vested, I show myself to the altar servers and gesture for their approval. Instead, their reaction is awe. I imagine my appearance is much like the angels intended, who dressed the Risen Christ in his tomb and sent their beloved back out into the world in a dazzling white robe. I face my deacons for the Mass with deference, whose vestments compliment mine, and in the next minute we are cued by the organist. We exit the sacristy and join the congregation.

The six of us gather at the front doors of the church, where we light the Paschal Fire, and I read aloud its Blessing. From this flame, I light the Easter Candle, a sign of the Resurrection of Jesus Christ, the Alpha and the Omega. Then, after lighting tapered candles, we process behind the deacon I have asked to chant prayers and carry the tall Paschal Candle into the dark church. The other servers stop at each pew alongside a parishioner to light their candle, and they in turn pass the light to the person next to them. When the deacons and servers finish and take their places within the sanctuary, including the deacon who has placed the Paschal Candle on a stand, we face the faithful. With all their candles burning bright and the final verse of The Exsultet is sung, I greet the faithful with the glorious announcement, "Christ is risen. Truly He is risen! Alleluia, Alleluia, Alleluia."

*As a part of the congregation, Laurel witnesses an unexpected miracle*

As Matt returns to his seat from the first reading, I am next. Standing up from my adjacent seat in the front pew, I move into the center of the aisle, bow in reverence, walk the steps up to the altar and off to the right to take my place at the pulpit for the second of several readings assigned. Although a lector for many years, on profound holy occasions such as tonight, I still get butterflies.

The Service of the Light which opens the Vigil and the Liturgy of Baptism which initiates new Catholics into the faith are added to the two principal parts of the Mass. The first part is called the Word of God and consists of four readings from Sacred Scripture. Three may be read by a lay lector. These parishioners are chosen in mind for their ability to read in public. The Gospel is read by the priest or deacon. The second part of the Mass is the Offertory, a sacerdotal function of the priest who consecrates the bread and wine which through the doctrine of transubstantiation is changed into the body and blood, soul and divinity, of Jesus Christ. Although this ritual must be performed by an ordained priest, this Holy Communion may be distributed to the congregation by those designated as Eucharistic Ministers.

Tonight and after the Liturgy of Baptism and the Word following the Sermon and the Prayers of the faithful, the priest begins the final part of the Mass, the Offertory. He is about two hours into the Vigil service. There is a slight swirl of activity off to my right which goes unchecked. Despite my airy front row seat, I know that the church is overcrowded with parishioners sitting close together and a bit overheated, but the glance of the celebrant during the elevation of the Host in that direction is so out of character, I have to divert my attention. Someone seems to have fainted in the pew directly across the aisle from mine. Before the Vigil, Ava and I were chatting and she was sitting in that area. I look to find her but cannot.

Suddenly, Father Leonardi stops the Mass to request in an urgent tone, "Is there a doctor in the house? Please, come up front."

The congregation is silent. A man walks briskly down the center aisle and passes in front of me in the direction where the celebrant points. Instinctively, I follow. Looking at who he attends to, I see Ava. Those around her are either fanning her face, fussing to unbutton her heavy coat, or cradling her head. Whatever the doctor is doing, Ava is unresponsive. He turns his head to one of the onlookers and commands, "Call an ambulance."

"Dear God, this is the Mass of the Resurrection!" In my despair, I look over to the priest at the altar shaking my head. He thinks of something and runs to the side of the sanctuary unlocking the Ambry cabinet where three blessed oils are kept, takes one, and runs with it over to Ava. He anoints her forehead with a prayer and in an instant, she opens her eyes. Miracles require witnesses, because people have to see them to believe. Coming out of it a little dazed but alive, he leaves her and in whatever emotion he is feeling resumes the Mass.

Until now, I just wanted him to be my Spiritual Director, because he replaced the former pastor, but this is for real. He just saved my friend, no less than on Easter.

---

*A duty of the pastor is to correct his ministers. Laurel accepts.*

The Easter holiday is exhausting particularly because it

51

follows Lent and Good Friday when Catholics who seldom come to confession often choose to avail themselves of the sacrament. Weeks and hours of extra time in the confessional booths with penitents, and no one to debrief us of what we hear due to our Seal of Confession are among the reasons we confess frequently. Priests will often say that their ears are the dirtiest part of their bodies. No parish priest is immune from this fatigue.

By my side my assistant shares in these duties. I can sense his stress and am empathetic. Fortunately, his mother wants to visit and the time is ideal to send him on vacation to unwind. When he returns, I will go on my own scheduled time off. Unlike any other season on the church Liturgical Calendar, Lent is a time when Catholics make a yearly confession for mortal sins. It is both a sad time for priests, who hear the accounts of terrible offenses, but uplifting in that a soul can be reconciled to God by accepting the salvation offered to them in the sacrament. Equally hard to hear are the intransigent venial sins from those we know or readily perceive: sins cultivated by the environment in which the community lives and are committed as easily on one person as the next. They are for covetousness of relationships and possessions, discouragement of faith by apathy or division, neglect of others to disgrace or cancel. We never intend to know who confesses what against whom within our parishes. We absolve God pardons, but the betrayal of a do-gooder can be impossible to avoid and unfortunate to mediate.

Still, I am diminished without those who serve. In the language of religion, such parishioners are in ministry with us. We are two priests here, serving a large parish with members homebound and terminally ill who ask that we bring them weekly Communion. The way we can be in all places is to designate Eucharistic Ministers who we call upon and come forward as neighbors.

"Yes, Elena. ...I understand. ...You made your point. ...I'm sorry you're upset. ...I'll have a talk with her. ...God Bless you, too. ...I hope you feel better. ...Call me anytime," I cut off line 1 and press line 2. "Donna, would you give me the phone number of Laurel Casey, please."

"Hello, may I speak with Laurel?"

"This is she."

"This is Father Leonardi."

"Hello, Father. To what do I owe the pleasure?"

Pity she sounds exuberant, "Laurel, can you stop by the rectory today?"

"Of course. I happen to be free now."

"Now is good. See you soon." You may think that she is unique in her degree of cooperation, but all my ministers drop what they are doing in their labors of love for God.

Before I fix my next cup of coffee, she has arrived. Donna gives her the go ahead and I greet her at the door to my office.

"What's the good word, Father?"

Again, there is that exuberance. I hate to deflate it. Seated behind my desk, she in front, I ease into the crux of our meeting with small talk but eventually have to get to the matter.

"How are your Communion calls going?" I think I am asking an open-ended question. She is new at this, but her reply is filled with concern for the other.

"Why, has anything happened to one of them? Is

everyone okay?"

My conversation with Laurel, regarding our homebound communicants, is private in the sense that we share a mutual respect for the dignity of the dying and their thoughts and agony in preparing to leave this world for the afterlife. This sacred trust can become skewed when the minister bringing Holy Communion to the parishioner is an old friend and unbelieving that the person has a diminished sense of reality.

For Elena, her conflict with Laurel is over her property. Since they first met, she knew Laurel to be a real estate agent. Her call to me is her fear that Laurel wants to sell her house; however, a person accused of trying to usurp the sale would be defensive, she is a compassionate listener.

"I had to bring her comments to light," I say as I finish relating them.

"My reputation is important to me. Not to confuse my priorities in anyone's mind, I let my sales license expire last year."

"You're not the first nor last of my Eucharistic Ministers to have a misunderstanding with a homebound parishioner. The people you visit are very sick, facing an imminent time for death. They think in terms of their final testimony in this world," Laurel listens attentively.

"I sat on the Chicago Realtors Ethics Committee. I can't think of taking advantage of anyone, let alone a sick friend. May I ask how I gave her that impression?"

I believe in her openness. "The diocese often has training on pastoral ministries. This work usually requires it and for such situations. Would you like to take a course when the next session starts? Instruction will build back your confidence, give you some dimension to the thought processes of the homebound."

"I can see good intentions aren't enough. I am one-hundred percent genuine in my feelings with people, bringing them the Eucharist or otherwise."

"Agreeing means you will curtail any worldly conversation, particularly about real estate?"

"Absolutely. I don't really know the feelings of a person in her condition. This is not my field of expertise but yours."

She agrees and that is all that matters at the moment. I am about to let her leave to think about the conversation, maybe even to stop into church and pray over it, when I am distracted by my intercom light flashing red. Excusing myself, I picked up the receiver.

"Father, you asked me to let you know immediately when Dominick and Louis arrived," my secretary tells me.

"Yes. We're ending our conversation. Please, send them in."

Instead of sending her out, I decide to introduce her to our parish seminarians to restore some of that feeling she walked in with.

"Dom, Lou! Come in. Sit," I greet them from behind my desk, pointing at the empty chairs next to my guest. "Do you know each other?"

"Yes. I'm Dominick. You're the lector on Thursdays. Nice to meet you," he extends his hand with a warm smile.

"I see you in church often with your parents," her smile returns.

"I'm Louis. My grandfather says you're the best lector."

The other seminarian reaches over to shake her hand. She laughs at the compliment, knowing otherwise.

"He and my grandma moved a long time ago, but they come with me to Sunday Mass when they visit. He also says he remembers you when your hair was long and straight down to your waist."

"Wow, what can I say? I was young once."

We all enjoy the spontaneous repartee. The brief conversation brings her back to her natural feelings rather than the deflated one, and she leaves feeling upbeat. Truth is, I pray God sends me people to help carry out my ministries. I take who He sends, but a more seasoned and less sophisticated minister than Laurel would have handled the Eucharist assignment better. There is a learning curve for everyone though.

---

*The difference between Laurel's spiritual and secular knowledge is noticed in her actions.*

Leaving his office, I made a visit to church. Within the hour, Rosa is having the alt-group over for lunch. If not so soon after my meeting with Father, I would research psychology articles relevant to the emotions of the dying and leave it at that. Instead, I blurt out his conversation over lunch and seek the good counsel of those with experience. Readily, the women come forward with their own mishaps over the homebound and times when the pastor had to intervene.

"I was so off-guard. I never thought of Father questioning my intentions. Truth is, I could stand instruction to understand what I am doing wrong. If a friend misunderstands me, I am in trouble."

"The homebound are in a different place mentally, not just physically, when we visit," Claire strengthens my new perspective. "Sometimes I think we're like angels who protect them. Bringing the Eucharist is a very powerful medicine not just for them but for those who live with them."

"The God squad, angel backup. Truth?" I hold up three fingers for a scout's salute "I did feel scrutinized, but he listened. When I thought about it, my friendship with Elena all these years was solely through the Rosarian Society."

"If she dies and her family lists her house with another Realtor, would you be offended?" Deanna challenges.

"Like I told Father, I let my license expire specifically to eliminate that perception. Even if I were asked, I couldn't. The fond memories I share with her have to do with our Rosarian fundraisers and at Mass. I feel privileged to know that after all the years in between, we have kept those memories alive."

"People believe what they want to about any one of us. They smile in your face and then stab you in the back in confession," Ava says frustrated.

"Step on you, like you're dead and then walk over you," Sophie exaggerates playfully.

"What if she had said something to Laurel instead of calling the pastor. They're friends. They could have talked it out. Why did she go through him? She's doing a good deed." Deanna waits and then answers rhetorically, "and that my friends is one reason why I am no longer involved with taking Communion calls."

## The Body and Blood

"In his defense, the dying are in an alternative state of mind. My communicants have memory loss, make up wild stories, hallucinate. It is not a matter of 'bring in the hypocrites.' They are sick," Claire defines the situation, well.

"I hear you, Deanna. I did say that I wanted to drop the ministry. He suggested I take a course on pastoral care. I love taking courses!"

"Don't you ever get tired of school? How old are you?" Ava and all of them laugh.

"School is an elixir for me."

"A what? An Alexa?" Rosa teases.

We're laughing and Mia tries to be funny and get in with her own joke.

"Did you ever see the walk?"

"Who are you talking about?" someone asks.

"Guess," she says standing up.

Our spirit is jolly and we accept the challenge. However, rather than laugh at me, which I opened myself up for, she begins to poke fun at the pastor. From mimicking his walk, she mimics his mannerisms, tone of voice, choice of words and intensions. Abruptly, I leave the room. Rosa follows.

"Come here," she says, grabbing my sleeve to pull me into her den. "What's wrong? Are you upset about what happened?"

"Not half as much as feeling guilty that I brought the conversation up, so someone could demean our pastor. I'm the one whose ego needed shrinking, why attack him? He wasn't insulting to me. The situation is between me and the communicant, and she is sick so I have to adjust. I find it distasteful when someone makes fun of other people. Poking fun at myself is fine, but when someone mimics someone to belittle them, I can't stand that. I've seen Mia do that before, particularly with priests. Did something happen to her with a priest? Someone close to her? There's something behind her behavior."

"She is who she is," Rosa is sad but ready to neutralize the behavior.

"Mia and I are building our friendship, so I'll leave my comments at that."

However, it isn't the last time she demeans a priest in a mocking manner and the next time it does happen, she is in much less sympathetic company than mine.

# 4

# *Legacy of a Mafia Parish*

*A pastor's sad duty and announcement.*

"Go and announce the gospel of the Lord," I conclude the Mass as I bless the congregation with the sign of the cross.

Leaving the sanctuary with my deacon and servers, we walk down the altar steps and I see the usual amount of people in the rear of the church scurry out to beat the Sunday 11 o'clock crowd to the parking lot. Good for them, but they will miss out on more than the cordial greetings among the parishioners who stay to the very end after this Mass.

Routinely and after, I turn and bow to the tabernacle, I turn back to the people, process up the aisle and outside where the congregation and I meet. Today, once the others have processed in front of me, I stop and ask everyone to, "Please sit. I have an announcement to make." There is complete compliance. "Thank you. Many of you have been asking me and are concerned about Father John. Until now, the Bishop has not given me permission to talk in public about his whereabouts and the circumstances surrounding his removal from the parish."

The silence is broken with the rustle of uneasiness. Anticipating their reaction, I remove my prepared notes from the sleeve of my vestment.

"Father John is not involved in any sexual infraction. However, he is accused of a serious matter the Bishop is required to examine. He will not be coming back to Immaculate Conception as my assistant. We are fortunate that the Bishop will be assigning us a replacement, who will join us soon."

I take in the full scope of the congregation and nod as if to agree with the sorrow on the faces I internalize. "This is a sad moment for us as a parish. I do not want you to take sides with the parishioners involved or with Father John. Differences arise between people and they are weighted and judged. In this instance a canonical process is required. We cannot jump to conclusions. Each member of our parish community is a part of the body of Christ. I also know that you revere your priest in a way that is ordained for him through Holy Orders in his priesthood. I ask you not to prompt me for details. Rather, I ask you to pray for those involved and for our parish. I have posted a letter in the bulletin in this regard. Thank you and from the bottom of my heart, I have faith that we will get through this in the peace and love of Christ. In the name of the Father and of the Son and of the Holy Spirit."

There is a hesitant "Amen" from the voices of nearly a full church in attendance. Noting their confusion, I change my mind not to greet them after such an announcement by my plan to walk directly into the sacristy. Instead, I face them outside in the bright sunlight of the church courtyard. Most are true to my request and enjoy the usual Sunday congeniality. That does not stop others who are overheard by my deacon, who discusses with me later bits and pieces of conversations with opinions and repercussions.

"Mia and her brother took their problem to the Bishop. Something about a health aide and their house," one man says.

"Father John is naïve about our culture and he was warned about their personalities," someone else says and gesticulates with his eyes raised to heaven and a slap to his forehead.

"It is their background," a person next to him finishes the thought.

"I am going to write a letter to the Bishop. No. I am going to start a petition," a young woman says to another young woman who singles out the word "petition."

"Where there's smoke, there's fire," the trite remark of a troublemaker.

"He's accused of something without a single family member in America to comfort him," says a woman who has several children.

I think to myself, thousands of miles away from home, he came to help us. My parishioners had embraced him as their own family. The siblings involved are family oriented, similar in their singularity and older than his parents, opened their home to him, ate with him, shared short trips. However, their emotions were far less endearing than those of his biological family. Mending differences, listening, compromising, finding common ground was not the approach that the siblings took to settle a difference of opinion. Even attempting to soothe the feelings between both parties in my office, in the presence of an adviser, there was no common ground. Theirs was the deepest cut of an ill-fated friendship: one that ended in revenge and scorn rather than disappointment and forgiveness.

In time, the gossip will fade and constructive conversation will take its place. Until then on one side or the other, or neutral, this matter will be talked about until it is resolved by the Bishop's Tribunal, a process which will take months or years to decide.

*Laurel, the former Realtor's opinion.*

Hurrying to do my chores after the 11, I manage to arrive a few minutes late at the Palmer House for the woman of the hour's birthday. Mia, who is at the center of the conundrum, will also be there. Ushered in by the hostess, I am waved on by our alt-group and join them at the dining room table and complete our number of seven. They are in the midst of listening to Deanna read the pastor's online letter from her iPhone. Claire puts her index finger to her lips to signal me, until the end of the message.

"While the canonical process selected to investigate the details of this matter involving the parishioners and Father John are being resolved, I ask you to pray for them and allow the truth to prevail. Yours in Christ, Father Michael Leonardi."

"Powerful thought," I comment, seeing faces too serious for a party. "You all look lovely, especially Sophie, a very Happy Birthday," I take the empty seat next to Mia with Claire on my other side.

"Turning this age is bearable in your company. Thank you," Sophie makes light of a certain age she is resistant to say.

"Okay, let's make our selections. Then, we can talk," Ava takes charge.

With our menus completed and in mid-course of our entrees', the real conversation commences.

"Was anyone at the 11 when Father made his announcement?" Claire asks, looking down at her food.

"I was," I say, mindlessly eating something on my plate

to allow others to talk.

"Richard and I went to the 11, so I could make the party. We thought the pastor handled it well. He had to say something. Father John is gone two months already."

"Claire came to the 11 with Paul and me. Paul was upset. Father John's been at our house a few times. They talk about sports."

"I went to the 8. A few people called me. They didn't understand, except it had nothing to do with sexual abuse," Ava rules out a scandal.

"Mia, I went to the 9:30. How are you and your brother holding up? This must be rough for you also," says Sophie softly, knowing we are all ears.

"Bob's okay. People in the parish have been asking us about what happened for weeks. He took so long to make it public."

"You mean, Father Leonardi?" Sophie asks.

"Him and the Bishop. We told both of them, my brother and I were wronged. All we wanted was a health aide. Father was helping us line up one for when we can't take care of ourselves. We have a Life Estate Deed in the name of the Church like you suggested, so we can die in our home. Our plan was to employ a middle-aged couple from Poland on a work visa. They could live in the apartment downstairs rent free and take care of us 'til the end."

"Mia, you're still healthy and just 70. An aide could be ten or twenty years off or never," Rosa appeals to her reasoning.

"My brother and I want to prepare, now."

"Okay, but when you had trouble doing that with Father John, why didn't you back off? Why did you involve your attorney and work to force the issue? Rosa's right, you didn't have to pressure Father. We could have helped you get what you wanted when the time came," Claire is firm.

"We have to prepare. I have to let my relatives know, my brother and I are taking care of our own business. All they want is our inheritance. We want to do with our money what we want."

"Calm down. We understand. You've told us. No one visits or invites you, but when you die they want your money. You don't have to be single and childless though to have relatives diminish your self-worth. Inheritance laws do that and you found a way around them. Smart cookies, I think. On the other hand, when things couldn't work out with Father for aides, why make him your Remainder? Most of all, why blame him when you changed your mind back to the original person you chose?" I say half in admiration and half in annoyance.

"He went along with it."

"Okay, you're both wrong, but it was your breach of contract. All the more reason to drop it," Ava says.

"Where there's a Will there's a way. Eventually, you would get what you wanted, just not with him," Deanna insists.

"She's right, Mia. You have friends, your ministries at the parish. Life is good," Rosa coaxes her.

"We could get sick any minute. We have to prepare. We have to have access to aides. Otherwise, we are one as in life, in death. It was working out until our plan fell apart and he pulled back. We don't want to leave anything to our relatives. They only call to ask if we're sick or to help them."

"Depressing," Ava says under her breath for most of us to hear.

"You have faith in God, Mia. You have so many blessings. You're overreacting. Even if you get sick suddenly, you have your brother. We're all here for you," Rosa says calmly. "You have insurance, room for a private nurse. Even when Father John would be reassigned, he would be a call away to help you, but not now. Priests don't litigate in court. You put him in trouble with the Bishop."

"We're not leaving our relatives any money. We're leaving it to the Church, so they have to help us."

"You made Father a friend and then when he couldn't help you and backed away, you decided to get him in trouble," Claire, their closest ally, calls them out. "You can't force him to produce aides, make some sort of legal arrangement by outmaneuvering relatives and the Church and when your plan falls apart, blame him. You're worried and upset about everything and bringing down the very people who are trying to help you."

"This is stinking thinking," says Ava worn out.

"Wait. Parts of their plan are interesting. The Life Estate Deed, the work visa, those allow the siblings to stay in their house with dependable help. One or the other would never be alone," I say.

"Wait. Wait up. Just a minute," Ava comes back. "You know perfectly well what you're doing. You want your house, your aides, and Father John all to yourselves. He's a priest who serves the entire community. You and your brother are selfish."

"Okay, this is my birthday. I like a discussion but not an argument. You invited me."

Sophie is rightfully annoyed. Our voices are raised and patrons have glanced over at the table a few times. We came to enjoy a friend's birthday. Fortunately, Deanna, who had excused herself from the table, returns with a trio of waiters. One pushes a table cart with a spectacular cake aglow with sparkler candles and a talented waiter able to sing Happy Birthday in a loud Baritone voice that ends the vitriol.

For the remainder of the party, the conversation over the incident has ended, but it is only the beginning of countless discussions among the women and the parishioners. The range of topics is hindered by the different introspection of the priest and these parishioners. The priest is revered for his type of self-sacrifice to God, while the siblings, without family and chaste, find their cross imposed and want more recognition for their generous participation in parish community: not just in eternity. Meeting up with one or more of my friends during the weeks ahead, we have a range of discussions to gain insight.

"I don't understand how their attorney allowed Father to participate in a legal transaction without his own representation?" Rosa asks me.

"Father's not a citizen yet, so I guess he trusted what everyone was doing. On the surface, it involved a legal transaction. Two clients paid their attorney to execute a real estate contract. It's business."

"What are your plans for old age? The siblings have a house and anticipate hiring a couple to live in their downstairs apartment and take care of them," Sophie asks me.

"Practical idea. Taking care of one or two people is a lot for one person, but to manage the upkeep of a house requires further help. After the super flood, we downsized to a condo. I made contingency plans with my attorney and a few trusted others to live out my life at home. God could change those plans. I have viable plans with options."

"What are you going to do to keep yourself occupied from now until then? The siblings have become recluses," Claire, who is the busiest regardless of age, asked.

"I am not as outdoorsy as you, but more so than the siblings. Besides, I'm always occupied constructively in parish life and studies. The siblings are not any different than us. There are a variety of ways to serve, if just in prayer," I challenge Claire to broaden her thinking on the different aims of charity.

"What did Father John give in return for their friendship? They were willing to give him their house," Deanna sees an imbalance in the relationship.

"I would say they made a wise choice. In return, Father would be there to say a funeral Mass and to bury one and then the other, and because they chose him to dispose of their earthly belongings, do that as well. However, what Father could not do was be their constant companion. They have to follow him, even if they walk together. We do at the 9, in our ministries, and membership in parish societies. Jesus left us a family in his Church. Even without a biological one in old age or at any age, there is an abundance of Church life."

"So what went wrong?" a choir of lovely ladies asks.

"I don't know. Except they did pull out of a contract. Father felt used or confused, pulled back his attention. They felt rejected not by the friend they made but by a priest, who they probably made their confessor besides. The priest was punished for a good deed. They messed up the friendship, but they wanted everyone to think he did."

"Him, just a little bit?" I'm challenged.

"I don't know. It's an old story. I guess."

Every story has a perspective. When corroborated truth prevails. No character, even a fictionalized one, is perfect. In this situation where one is an ordained priest whose time spent with friends is limited to the call of his pastor to assist him in serving the common causes of many, and the other side is a brother and sister frightened out of their wits, human decency did not prevail. The underlying desires of the siblings were unmet, because the giver was restricted in giving what they wanted, and their gifts were for that reason superfluous. As a Catholic raised and schooled in my religion since before I was knit in my mother's womb, I am aware of reform movements. They are indeed epic. Except for the Church's hypervigilance in a post-scandalous era, this squabble would have been handled for the good of all.

---

*Laurel is undecided and visits her psychologist mentor.*

An interesting thing about my retirement is that I didn't have to think about what I would do on the first day of it. My morning would start the same way it had in the past nearly five decades with Mass. Whether I worked in the Loop, or out in the suburbs, or at my alma mater, or in the neighborhood, I found a Catholic Church to attend a weekday Mass a practice began after a divorce.

So what is the rest of a typical day for me? Five years later, with the presence of my mom's aide from 8:30 AM to 1:30 PM, the remainder of her day is spent in my care. In her early-90s, she remains interesting to share with and her health issues challenge me to learn about all kinds of things. An only child, I know how best to keep my down time occupied. Life is manageable. So, why had a communicant misunderstood me, and how could I be involved in a group where siblings are at the root cause of a priest possibly losing his vocation? Without a Spiritual Advisor, I reach out to an old psychologist mentor.

"Dr. Napolitano," I'm happy to say as he greets me at the door to his office. "It's great to see you."

"It's been ages. You look the same, Laurel," he mirrors my smile and we accept the mutual admiration between academics, who delight in exercising their talents. "Please, come in," he leads the way and points to a chair opposite to where he will sit. "I'm flattered you thought of me to discuss your dilemma, but it's not novel for you."

"I feel entangled between arguments I have nothing to do with. The past several weeks have been wretched. I haven't felt this downcast since I went through a divorce," I sigh.

"And what did you do to relieve yourself of those feelings?"

"Two things. First, I prayed and read books by saints like nobody before and a few years later, I returned to college for a second career."

"Which helped more?"

"Hard to say. I combined them. I kept up with daily Mass and went to a Catholic University, staying as far away from the world of fashion as I could," I laugh at the ill-match of my former college discipline.

"You did, didn't you," he gives an understanding look knowing this background from his mentorship. "In reality both choices became one, an interesting salvation story. Is that why you want to return to DePaul? No one is ever too old to learn. It is unusual for someone your age, but with online courses doable."

"I agree, but what do I study?"

"The way to decide depends on why you feel your parish is no longer a safe haven?"

"Church was but hasn't been a good place for me recently. I make allowances for where I live and the parish I'm in. My neighborhood has everything to offer with an Italian flavor, but I'm taken for Irish. Certain Sicilians tend to be clannish," I stop to associate a memory. "On visiting days, my dad would say that my maternal Italian side might get to raise me, but I would always have his name and the map of Ireland on my face. Turns out he was right."

"All these years, I even thought you were all Irish. Half and half. Your father was sharp. As for parishes in general, some are more biased towards one nationality or race than another. There are lots of reasons for it. Think of the Euro-Catholic nations that founded The New World, and the European missionaries who established the religion from west to east coasts and in the Gulf. That filtered down to neighborhoods that self-segregated by ethnicity, race, and even religion aside from economic social classes. What nationality are the priests?"

"The pastor is Italian, the assistant was Polish, and the replacement is now an Italian."

"From what you explained over the phone, you feel nationality is why you're caught in the middle."

"If I were to narrow my problem to one, yes. I cope. I have my own little world of things to do with my mom and pastimes, but since retirement I've reached out for parish people, some new and some who I casually knew for 40 years. I found a group I identify with as childless. We meet for breakfast at the diner. We're sensible. The relationship has led to luncheons, birthdays, and holiday socials, which on occasion includes my mom. We reciprocate. I've been invited to join various religious groups, but my time is preoccupied."

"Exactly how does your feeling of ethnic discrimination dominate your thoughts? You sound accepted in your circles of friends."

"The problem is over a priest in our parish, who came here from Poland. He was invited in and became friendly with a woman in my alt-group and with her brother. The relationship ended but the aftermath shook me up. The Bishop removed the priest from our parish. It was such an overreaction, it scared me."

"The cause and effect does seem extreme from a disagreement to revenge. Theirs is a private matter. It doesn't involve you."

"True. What frightens me is how quickly a small matter jumps into a huge one. There is an odd sense of communication lacking between people that takes place instead with the priest in the confessional. Rather than confronting the person themselves, the very person who they share a friendship with, they talk about him in confession. I'm unaccustomed to this type of avoidance. It seems mean-spirited, like what happened to Father John. Behind his back, the siblings mocked him, were over critical and crushed the spirit out of him. If you don't like someone why does a person have to involve God? It seems to me a constant grinding down of people for the sake of grinding them down, pitting Catholic against Catholic. The pastor has been diplomatic with homilies that stick to the text, but you can tell he is sad about losing his assistant yet adamant about protecting the two souls involved. Many parishioners feel a cathartic ending to the tension. However, I imagine from the reaction of the siblings theirs is more of a priestly purification for wrong thinking. What protects me is apparently grace gained from my training to analyze and write about my emotions and the good sense to seek your counsel. Why do we do this to one another?"

"Culture, nurture. Apart from religion, culture plays a major role in how a person is raised."

"Why? Because he is Polish. This is a priest who needs an advocate."

"Why you? Because your stepfather was Polish?" he sees me in the middle.

"Probably that and years of being around good priests. My new friends talk about the situation constantly. I can't get it out of my head, and I feel for everyone involved."

"Diocesans are different from Order priests. Religious orders tend to be less diversified and their priests are more concentrated to a particular geographical region and nationality. The Church is going through a rough patch. There is a supply and demand for Diocesans priests who generally blend into the local community. You might be right, given who replaced the priest."

"It is terrible to listen to people when they generalize the bad with the good. We're crucifying them all? You can hear the tension come across from the pastor. He says that all it takes is one phone call and he's out. I'm embarrassed by that insecurity. We can do better by our priests. I can write a book or something?" I feel a well of emotion come up in me.

"That feeling you have, own it. That's why this dilemma isn't novel for you. It happened before, when your internship at the rehab ended and you continued to work there. Why? Because it was run by a priest, and you saw his work as saintly. You wanted to improve how the therapeutic community handled rehabilitation. Laurel, you changed your major from psychology to theology. You crossed over into their world of religion. You had dual roles. It was hard to figure out which one you were acting in. Eventually, management accepted your hypothesis, but not you so much. Why? You weren't a consecrated religious or a former client. The priest was on their side, and fortunately we, the University, was on yours. Your idea for a Spiritual Survey spread in the classroom, interest was generated, papers were written. Eventually, psychologists implemented a version. Drug abusers who reform have earned the right to be fully reintegrated into society, as well as into a particular religion, including the Catholic Church. And now you're here to ask for my advice of which course you should take. You know which one. Take it" he says amused knowing me better than myself.

"This is a free session, isn't it? You're so smart and I'm still in agony."

"Laurel? Do you know why religious let you cross back and forth the way you do? You're a natural and a licensed professional. You love people, they love people, except this time you are both nestled in a parish arena."

I stay silent, eager to gain insight about myself.

"Before, when you conducted research, you had the psychology and theology departments plus your priest friends to protect you. Now, you're in a parish alone. Let me ask you this, do you see them for their sins or for their data?"

"Sins."

"Does that give you an answer to your dilemma, I hope?"

"Theology?"

"You have the same altruistic trait you had years ago, I am here for you," he says getting up to indicate the session is over and walking to the door with me in tow says, "Give my regards to your mother. Keep in touch. Send me your book," with a smile that matches mine.

"You're the greatest."

"You're the best," he winks back as I take my cue and leave.

---

*Father Mike. Saturday afternoon parish confessions.*

It is a contradiction in terms to ask me, a parish priest, "Did you have a restful weekend?" When God told the Hebrews and through them our bloodline to celebrate him on the Sabbath, he meant for his priestly servants and their staff to give Him homage every week. On the Saturday afternoon preceding our Sabbath, Catholics are invited to examine their consciences and purify their souls. It is noon; I wait for whomever comes into the confessional Booth.

"Bless me Father for I have sinned," is the prayer of humility that begins every confession, followed by "Forgive me my sin of" any commission of the Ten Commandments, and for Catholics any omission of the Eight Beatitudes. We are under a binding Seal of Confession which surpasses any professional code of secrecy. Nevertheless, there are penitents, the most famous among them being St. Augustine, in his *Confessions*, who reveal their sins to others, in a gesture of vulnerability. I will let their books speak for themselves.

"Bless me Father for I have sinned. I love the siblings but they are too much for me. I am worn out with their problems. I want to be there for all my friends, but their talking goes on and on, hours. Forgive me, but I have to spread myself around, as well as, take care of myself."

"Bless me Father for I have sinned. I love the siblings, and I feel awful about giving up on them, but they don't stop talking about Father John. I am sorry for getting in between them and thinking I could mediate. God is so in charge on this one."

"Bless me Father for I have sinned. I love the siblings, but they are too time consuming. I multitask in this parish, run my household, and socialize with my family. Every time I think I have helped them resolve their issues, they come back with new ones or the same ones undone. All they want is to reopen old wounds until they are in the right. I have to spread myself around."

"Bless me Father for I have sinned. I love the siblings, but they are too stressful for my friends and me. We are getting older and our issues are health, that we manage with doctors. Their issues are priests and Father John. For the good of the whole and my psyche, I have to separate myself from them."

"Bless me Father for I have sinned. I love the siblings, but this melodrama is not me. I can't believe Father John is so tangled up in them. He reminds me of the Laocoon and his sons statue. I cannot befriend anyone if they want to force a priest out of the priesthood without just cause or if fellow priests have to disassociate with a priest who has journeyed thousands of miles to join us and possibly lose his vocation in the process. I know that is happening, but I don't understand why. I've seen how you take charge. My sin is not to become involved in matters of the Church unless I understand how to become involved."

"Bless me Father for I have sinned. I love people, but gossips and those who mock others can just as easily hurt me as well. Amen."

By the end of hearing confession for two hours, the problem becomes obvious and seems to have temporarily solved itself. Parishioners have decided to step back. My assistant, who I shared the parish rectory with for two years, the priest sent by our Bishop's Office, who helped me minister to our people of God and prayed for every intention we asked of him, was no longer. I tried everything to keep him. My lips are sealed. The decision belongs to the Bishop. I feel compassion for both sides.

# 5

# Spiritual Advisors

*Father Mike. Lunch out with Father Mark a conflict and a confrontation in ministry.*

Living in an upper class neighborhood, I am invited to many parties. Rarely do I have time to go. Why? I am busy throwing my own annual and impromptu celebrations that take place on our church grounds for sacraments, school and ministry events. One such dinner party is for the twentieth anniversary of my priestly ordination. A similar celebration is the one my Spiritual Director invites me to. I would hardly be here without him.

Like anyone, there are personal and work challenges in my vocation. Without the mentorship of Father Mark, the outcome of these tests of faith would have been poorly mastered. Granted, I am not an easy man to cope with in a short-term relationship, so often I defer to his judgment. Two people in my life mean more to me than my parents: he is one of them. For this occasion, our Thursday meeting in his parish office has been moved up and shifted to a dinner out at a five-star restaurant.

"Have you ever been to the River Park before?" Mark asks me as we take a window seat and place our dinner napkins on our lap. "This view of the Randolph Bridge gives me pause to pray for the hundreds who died fleeing the Fire from the other side. I come here once, twice a year and I have the same staggering feeling every time."

"My great great-grand uncle was here in 1871. He lived in the Old St. Patrick parish. He and his brothers became part of the Great Rebuilding. Hardy Italian stock, they were."

"We both know you were assigned to your parish because of your Italian background, but do you find it essential or helpful?"

Mark has taken an abrupt turn in the conversation. My thoughts were set to elaborate on my family's Chicago roots, his from a predetermined perspective. I begin my answer picking up on his word, "Essential. I'm not my predecessor who had three priest assistants and a convent of six nuns. Raised in an Italian family with a litany of relatives, my maternal American Revolutionary roots are a detraction. Relationships took Monsignor's staff of mixed nationalities months and years to cultivate. They take to me in no time. A one-to-one for ten-minutes in the middle of a noisy wedding, I have a landsman for life," he looks puzzled. I check myself, "Excuse me, for the sake of the Church."

"Is that why your assistant from Poland failed to work out?"

His question is leading. When going through the circumstances around my assistant's removal, my Spiritual Director was a tremendous help. When arbitrating between both parties, he would tell me, 'Don't talk. Listen. Bring in a staff member as a witness. Don't let the priest and siblings confront one another,' that was, of course, after I made that mistake. 'Tell the parishioners, it is a Church matter that the Bishop is handling. Make yourself the solution, not part of the problem.' That said, he wants reasons how this could happen. He sounds more loyal to the Bishop, and probably is, than to me. Why not? He is the other person we both respect most in our lives. "We are talking about a priest who is ordained as long as you and his vocation to our Holy Mother Church is in jeopardy."

"I have a theory but yes, the problem got out of hand. I assume responsibility."

"Let me speak in terms of priest shortage and Catholic demographics. The dynamics of our parishes are rooted in particular nationalities and races. A priest who reflects the culture of his parish or adapts to it, wins the hearts of people. Your Italian neighborhood has good and, let me be kind, wayward people in it, within the same household, and a generation removed with monies from ill-gotten gains. Some individuals rose above that background with significant accomplishments and others plateaued or succumbed to crime. Regardless, all are proud of their Italian heritage and inheritances. They don't want to be Polish. Do I make my point?"

"On the other hand, John is accomplished and fully Polish. We have a recent pope who became a saint from Poland. The religion is universal. Both nationalities are proud," I reinforce his assessment and share my thoughts further. "From what I hear, they've all moved, a few goodfellas remain, but their once large crime syndicate is gone. I doubt he broke the Seal of confession. Language is mostly nonverbal. People figure things out. This priest might have known the basics of the Mafia, but the nature and nurture aspects of children raised in their home life, which goes for anyone's upbringing, no. Not until it became personal did he react, whether that grew out of confessions or unsettling conversations or both. We're priests, not psychologists debriefed on personalities and who write research papers based on statistics or cops backed by arrests and courts records easily Googled. I struggle as well between the mystery of God and worldly knowledge."

# The Body and Blood

"You have me as your confessor and you have the pulpit. What's the problem?"

"You know my confessions. In my homilies, I approach the concept of family from the holy dynamic of parents and their children. I talk about their security and advancement by knitting them even closer through our Catholic values. That the obedience of the Son to the Father proceeds through their Holy Spirit, not from the knowledge of God according to Adam and Eve. My parishioners are hard workers whose properties took a major hit in a super flood. Some moved, others bounced back. Their money grew from real estate and investments, nothing to do with crime. I accept the good with the bad. Probably, there was a guy who went to Father John. Don't you remember as a kid how many of a certain type went to the priest who might not have caught their every word? Well, they underestimated him: John heard and understood every word. In the rectory, we talked in generalities. Our schedules were vastly different. Murder is a tough confession to absolve and mete out a penance. You know this."

"The demands on you—two and now one priest—for thousands of people with the obligation and the desire to recruit more men to the priesthood is not the light burden Christ promised you 20 years ago when you were ordained. I'm sorry Mike."

He has given me an answer, but one that must be fulfilled rather than changed.

"Thank God for your lay ministers. The vision to install them by the See was providential," and finished with our meal, he places his payment card in the billfold the waiter has set at his side of the table.

Returning with his card and receipt to sign, the waiter

turns to me and asks, "Are you a Catholic priest, Reverend?"

It is obvious. I am wearing my clerical suit. With no reason to think amiss about my response, I say with a warm smile, "Yes, 20 years."

He cups his hand to whisper in my ear, "Are you a pedophile too? Your sort ruined my brother."

Having said what he wants I stand straight up but wait for the rage within me to simmer. Without a context for the guests in the restaurant to know what he said, I would look in the wrong. I have learned to check my temper and count to five. Mark reacts to the non-verbal exchange and gets out of his chair, taking me by the elbow to lead me out as quickly as my count reaches three. I can't say what I would have done at five.

"Do you see why I didn't wear my collar. This is what we are up against. I'm surprised it hasn't happened to you before. Keep walking and wait to talk until we're outside. Say some prayers," he says distracting me.

It seems like a minute. We are out in the fresh air. I am able to take in a few deep breaths. Then, I unleash hell on the guy. I hadn't allowed myself to curse in a good long while, but today set me back to day one. Mark keeps pulling me away from the front of the chic restaurant with a doorman and valet who smirk with the sound of my words in contrast to their pent up ones. Reaching a bench, he pushes me hard enough that I stumble into the seat.

"You finished? You got all that bile out of your belly? Who's the greater fool, him or you? Come to your senses and collect yourself."

Sorry that I have upset him, I force myself to come out of my angry daze. "Have you had that happen? Do you know priests who experienced that?"

"A few. What do you think we're up against just words? Hell no. People who have been victims, relatives and friends of victims, regular and marginalized Catholics and non-Catholics. Mike, your parish problems have reasons and those reasons are in combat with your mission to attract vocations."

Tearing my collar off, I say "I'm not wearing this out in public."

"Oh, yes you are but not this public, your parish, your neighborhood, among people who want you to earn their respect. That's where you will wear your collar. You have a community of believers, and you have a core group. It's your 9 o'clock attendees. It's your school parents. It's your ministers. You wear your collar and the more you do, the more confidence you give them that we stand together for a religion with a two-thousand-year history. One that endured the jaws of lions, persecutions of governments, betrayers among our own. You belong to God and his people. Take this waiter's insults, but digest your parishioners' hurt and pain from the humiliations they endure as Catholics from family and friends and colleagues at work. They take the brunt of wounded souls like that waiter just handed you, but they endure. Your burden is light compared to theirs. You are not seeing the whole picture. You have to raise your sights. You've got a free ticket provided you don't mess it up like your Assistant," he warns menacingly. "None of us like what happened to John. None of us."

"I tried. Honestly, even with mediators in the room with us. The siblings are scared out of their minds with what will happen if they're sick, or another flood happens, and then if one of them dies before the other," I reflect on their fixations. "Actually, they had a good idea using John to procure a Polish aide on a work visa. It got twisted. They wanted his constant attention. He has duties tied to the school, the parish, his ministries. It was getting out of hand. It's not like I didn't personally help them."

"There are a lot of variables at play with John. One God, One Scripture, One Mass, but many cultures: The Tower of Babel. God keeps us chasing him for sure. John has a big heart coming here to help us, and this is the deed he is sacrificed for. This is not only about the nature of the siblings, it is about the priest and their clashes in culture. That there was an unwillingness for him to surrender to God is on us," Mark is discouraged.

"There might be something hopeful," I am desperate to come up with an idea. "A parishioner came to me with a business proposal that might work readjusted to a religious mission."

"That's the kind of thinking you have to have. Use what is in your circle, your City of God!"

"Augustine's pretty cool. Even the waiter would have to admit that if he read him."

"Use what you have," Mark clicks his tongue with a thumbs-up.

---

*Laurel. One foot in her beloved parish and the other on the rich soil of her alma mater.*

"Yes, Father Dara is expecting you. Follow me please," the faculty hostess escorts me past other tables with faces here and there I recognize but who are too engrossed in conversation for me to catch their eye. I have a feeling of homecoming.

"Laurel," Father teeters to stand, but with our wide smiles that match how happy we are to see one another the significant difference in our ages is unnoticed. "Everyone, this is Dr. Casey and friend of many of our Vincentians dearly departed and the one remaining from their era," he says, taking my hand, and in his amusing manner he kisses the back of his. We chuckle at his felicity. "Allow me, this is Father Newman, chair of the theology department, Father Lewis philosophy, and Dr. Carroll, your former political science teacher, he tells us."

From the "greetings" to the "see you all again," I am delighted to share in their company, to reminisce in stories of battles of wits played out in the academic arena with words from books we study and those we write. However, I am there to see Father Dara in private, and when the five of us finish our lunch, the three professors leave, and he and I stay to finish our dessert and conversation.

"Did you ever learn anything about your stepfather?" he asks the same question everyone does who I haven't seen in a long time.

"Nothing, Father. I am afraid my mother and I will have to wait for the afterlife for that prayer to be answered."

"I was always struck by the coincidences surrounding that event. I believe you were working as an intern at a drug rehab run by a priest, a Monsignor."

"He was a special diocesan."

"And with our Dr. Napolitano?" He knows my link to the university.

"Eventually. We compiled data on intelligence and depression measurements. I tested intakes admitted to rehab and retested them three months after treatment. Eighty-five percent effective."

"Good work."

"I admired his program, but I loved the experience of the study more."

"Father Peter?" he smiles knowing another link plus a friendship.

"A remarkable sociologist. I could never have understood the mindset of imprisoned criminals without his guidance."

"What about Monsignor?"

"Amazing journey. He wrote about it. Did you know the Church started him off with unused retreat houses to open his rehab?" Father is relaxed and interested. "First in Chicago, and then out in the burbs. Their therapy is group. As an intake interviewer, I gathered information to identify clients' major issues triggering drug abuse. After a while, my interests drifted. Not one adolescent practiced a religion. Not one. I became focused on how the whole process of reform started for them by a priest absent this spiritual component."

"Why did you leave?"

"Father Peter died. I had no one to debrief me. My detour into theology to write a Spiritual Survey instrument went nowhere. Correction," I rephrase my statement. "It went nowhere with me. The leadership under Monsignor was absolute. Those who returned after rehabilitation to serve, choose their own version of spirituality, usually focused on health and exercise. I left and went into education and earned my doctorate in that field. I'm retired for a couple years."

"I recall you had an unusual reunion with your

biological father during that time through Anna, one of our house secretaries."

"Yes. It felt beyond a coincidence. As soon as we recognized one another, she called my dad and after thirty years we reunited. He was remarried to a woman who had previously been married to a Catholic. I helped her through an annulment process. They remarried in the Church, and he died a few years after. My mother and stepfather were good with it. Father Peter not so much."

"Peter had been hurt for you. But then, your stepfather went missing."

"He did," I am speechless, reminiscing the chain of events.

"The timing impressed me. I just never forgot it, more like plummeting the depths of God."

"Nor have I. Within a year following this reunion, Frank disappeared and Father Peter died. My car was stolen and a week later its replacement was stolen as well. Where I worked, I heard of murder but mostly of kids stealing cars all the time. So I missed sight of something dangerous going on in my mom's business. Without realizing, she hired and trusted a wanna-be type."

"Wanna-be?"

"Mafia. They determine their own sort of beliefs and rituals," I infer a stereotype, the antithesis of ours inspired. "Her agent was ambitious, so my mom sent him for executive real estate training in Las Vegas of all places. Instead of attending the meetings, he went to the casinos and had the nerve to tell her. She let him go. A few weeks later, the stolen cars and Frank's disappearance," The scenario makes the priest uncomfortable. He leans forward and taps the top of my hand resting nearest to him.

"I knew there was something. Our confrere Peter taught criminology. You have to be careful with that element."

"I am, and I have been," I wonder if I should have confided in him. He is the only Vincentian of that time period I have left. "Father, I received a card a few months ago from a Mafia Don," I whisper the surname. "Since I'm retired I have had time to reflect on Frank's death. It seems obvious he was killed by them. Maybe even this man."

The priest is calm, but tense in his body language. He no longer wants to carry on such a conversation in the faculty lounge.

"Help me up, Laurel. Let's visit the church."

Once outside, walking the immaculate grounds of the campus, it is a beautiful sun filled day with trees 120 years old in full bloom and grass as green as emerald. We talk about our faith, old age, Christ and his Mother and foster Father and the kind of afterlife he longs for as I do. He wants me to know the difference between self-righteousness and righteousness, and I listen. I say that it is not about holiness versus sinfulness, rather our ministries versus their arrogance. This man or men who murdered Frank might have been given absolution in confession and deliberately sought distribution of Holy Communion from my mother. His children might have been instructed by her in the parish religious ed after school program. Those are the thoughts I find hard to dismiss. I have no interest in revenge or self-righteous indignation. The point Father understands and why he hears my confession when we are in Church is that the murderer seems to be pursuing me.

"Stay honest, Laurel. Follow the example of your mother. Even in her state of mind, she remains committed to her dreams for you. She raised you along with her mother through their honest labor. You are a highly educated student of ours and humble because of your Catholic training and confident in your friends here. This is a rare combination that you alone possess. Value it. You have increased not decreased in knowledge and grace. Legitimacy is what they want but refuse to earn. Lacking contrition, they can't accomplish what others with good reputations can.

Their one recourse is to ask God to forgive their sins, but their record is repeated murders. You ask the intercession of saints and angels to follow the way of Christ. They beg the absolution of priests after committing crimes with made-men, but then, refusing to learn from created-men. He gave us two commandments, one of agape and one of philia, love of God and of man. With absolute confidence first, love God and second, love your neighbor as yourself. His words are eternal."

"How can I love my neighbor, a parishioner, if he has killed my stepfather? That would mean I would accept the same to happen to me and forgive the person who did so, if he receives absolution from a priest. That's impossible, Father."

"Do you love Our Savior?"

"I do. I love Christ in humility."

"Then, my child, you can do what he has. You are an example of the love Jesus showed his Father for the redemption of us all. On the cross, he forgave his murderers, because they lacked the gift of grace given to you. Through your wisdom and in your innocence, they want you as well as their creator to redeem them. I believe you are righteous to expose him, if he is the man who killed your stepfather. Be careful. Only God can give this man the divine forgiveness he seeks. He is tortured by his own undoing. 'Revenge is mine sayeth the Lord.' I am concerned for your safety. Let us pray the Our Father."

Together we start by making the sign of the cross.

"Our Father who art in heaven hallowed be Thy name. Thy Kingdom come. Thy will be done on earth as it is in Heaven. Give us this day our daily bread and forgive us our trespasses as we forgive those who trespass against us, and lead us not into temptation but deliver us from evil. Amen."

This moment with him is vivid, as if a picture hung on my wall. Whatever happens to me, the faith Father Dara represents transcends my mother's fears and my doubts to publish.

# 6

# *Rebuilding the Church*

The mystery of the body and blood of Jesus Christ, truly God and truly Man, is evident in the Holy Communion between the priest and the congregation. To reduce a doctrine as powerful as this into one sentence is not to diminish its significance, rather it is to make the message as clear as possible. The people of the Catholic Church and our priests are undivided. They have to do something unthinkable for us to give up a single one, and we pray vice versa. The recent pedophile scandal is such an historical instance. Even the tolerant laity, priests and popes yell out, "Enough." Yet, this is how our socially just religion acts.

---

*There is no substitute for a Catholic priest and he is hard to find.*

Setting aside the distinction between Diocesan and Order priests over the past fifty years in the United States, the decline in vocations is more than fifty percent. Among women entering the religious life as nuns or sisters the decline is seventy-five percent. Strict vows of behavior that include celibacy, obedience, and poverty for those who join Saintly Orders, have always been deterrents during periods when the numbers of priests and sisters increased. So what changed? For one thing, the laity does not want to support those in religious life who fail to model appropriate behavior. For another, men and women discerning a vocation to the religious life realize their vows are hard to keep and the world is transparent. Everybody knows everything.

Are there alternatives? Lay ministers, apart from ordained Deacons, have been one solution, but as this story reveals there can be terrible consequences involved. To say one is a forgiving person in order to minister to others, without reservation to one's family and oneself, this is impossible without extraordinary grace from God. It may very well be the reason why Jesus speaks of followers who are spiritual relatives in nature, the gravitas of redemption. Conversely, to say that God has a Last Judgment in order to enter heaven might sound fair until one realizes that, some Catholics choose to be reckless in their behavior about sin until their last confession, so to speak or rely on various indulgences to keep them out of Hell at least. Therefore, during this period of reformation to restore the priesthood to its numbers for a more vibrant life of the Church, the solution of lay ministers is supplementary at most.

Catholics know this. They also understand that a vocational calling is rare and the expectations of a priest once in ministry will be challenging.

For example, Diocesan priests manage the overhead and operation of their parish which often includes an elementary school. If you own a house, magnify the cost of maintenance and staff upwards to the size of a large church. If you are involved in the education of young children, fathom your hopes and aspirations for them, times hundreds of children, knowing they are yours to teach in the faith but maybe not all to keep.

If he is an Order priest a vow of poverty in surrender to his mission is included. You want priests who are high school educators and university professors to teach theories in the fields of humanities and sciences for the advancement of the Kingdom of God, not for self-remuneration or vainglory. You want your charities to be supervised by priests in the trenches with the poor and the afflicted, rather than philanthropists far afield and for a tax shelter. You want Chaplains in prisons, on battlefields, in hospitals, armed with the words and balm of a heavenly purpose for those who suffer.

Overall, you want all priests to be this capable and to pray fervently to live up to these ministries. Regularly, priests acknowledge their sinfulness, very aware of how important it is to live up to a moral code. Their caveat is if they fail to an extreme, regardless of their age or means, they will be to various extents expelled. Is it any wonder why they ought to be celibate? Why they should be obedient to rules they barely have time to ponder but for valid reasons accept and follow?

Yes, their goal to sit at the right hand of God is worth the test. Priests believe this with their heart, mind, soul, and strength, but they know full well no person escapes temptations and the best of mortals are fallen sinners.

Certainly, professors and students of theology are passionately in tune with the centrality of the priesthood. Without them, there is no Catholic Church.

---

*Women priests are not the solution.*

I begin my next course and meet the professor for The Sacrament of Matrimony in a Zoom chat. It is a delight to have a conversation with her as we share in common the memory of so many people from the university over a span of forty years, including a legacy of those souls dearly departed or who have moved on to retirement or other academic venues.

"Did you know many of the Vincentians?" I ask the cheery, youthful looking professor who shares the video call with me in lieu of an office meeting.

"My mother did. She went on a couple of alumni trips with Fathers who were hosts. Very normal priests," she sounds certain.

Her description amuses me, but I pass on it.

"That's how I came to know them, outside of class on alumni trips in the late 80s and 90s. They were fun with interesting life experiences to share," I say thinking this is what she means by normal.

"Those priests were usually the university administrators, rather than the faculty."

"I guess. I didn't stop to think about that, but you're right. My closest priest friend, in his 80s, taught as well."

"My Vincentian friends were colleagues in the Theology Department. Father Cleary was closest to me. He married Charles and me, baptized our children. They were normal," she stresses the adjective again.

"I almost canceled my first pilgrimage. My mom couldn't go but she and my stepdad encouraged me. I was getting over a divorce and annulment. The priests lifted my spirit and made me their friend. Of course, I wanted to become a nun and they helped me. No nunnery wanted me. Maybe I was too old, mid-30s or the divorce slash annulment. Also, I'm an only child and so is my mom. The nuns were always thinking ahead. Instead, I decided to work for the Church and wound-up studying psychology or was it the other way around? Work and school are so intertwined for me sometimes."

"So you know what I mean when I say normal. Those priests were very normal."

She is making the same point that eludes me. "The priests were as close as brothers, but like I said one, Father Peter, became a friend of mine and my family for over ten years. He was older than my stepfather," I say this to suggest an age distinction. "We were sometimes father daughter, peers, mentor and student, or two prayerful Catholics: never confessor and penitent. I felt that confessing my sins to Father would spoil our friendship. I had a Spiritual Director."

"Those were the days. My husband and I were active in every facet of Catholic life. Not all priests are alike."

Again she leaves off in a way I don't understand. I take another guess. "A priest I knew for years was accused of pedophilia but exonerated and died shortly after."

"There is that and other issues to look at with priests these days."

"I hear you. Honestly I do. My experiences are different. I discuss this topic with other Catholics. Everyone seems to know someone who has been accused. We are sad, hurt, and disappointed. We share similar feelings about these scandals. We know that good priests suffer the wicked priests in different ways than us. The contrast is they persevere, overcome their temptations to leave the Church, and stay with us. An example of good conquering evil. You counsel married couples?"

"I counsel them as one. These are troubled marriages and between them, there is usually one with a sexual dysfunction from childhood."

"My concentration was drug rehabilitation and the probability of sexual, physical, or verbal abuse as a child was a given. Yet, in over a thousand cases I worked, none involved a priest," I say trying to underscore the secular side. She is silent and I think to disclose something. "Just as the men in the priesthood are one, together we form the mystical union of Christ, like in a marriage the two are one. May I be personal?"

"Yes, of course."

"I know this may sound awful but if I had to go through the terrible marriage I did to meet Father Peter and his Vincentian brothers, I would. Next to my mother, he was the kindest, most genuine person I ever met," I am saddened by my admission.

"The other ones did a lot of damage to the Church, Laurel. They hurt us more than they gave."

"Even in the long run? You are overlooking all the normal ones," I want to help her put the wrong image behind her, but her responses leave me to think she cannot. Some viewpoints require time to unfold. I respect her intellect and value her insights as one of my many teachers. Moreover, she is a woman men are attracted to and their daughters are proud of, but on this one point we disagree and take it up in our scholarship.

She advocates women in the Catholic priesthood and if not, then in a Christian priesthood.

---

*Young Catholics empowered with Gifts of the Holy Spirit can rebuild the Church.*

For members of the Catholic faith, there are major turning points in their religious lives. Beginning with their initiation through the indelible sacrament of Baptism, followed by the sacraments of Reconciliation and Holy Communion, and then Confirmation, which without Matrimony and Holy Order would be the final sacrament unless Last Rites are given. Confirmation is generally received by young adolescents who have been schooled in a religious instruction program. This great sacrament fortifies a teenager with a can-do spirit of seven virtues called the Gifts of the Holy Spirit: Wisdom, Understanding, Counsel, Fortitude, Knowledge, Piety, Fear of the Lord. The power of these super virtues take on an additional meaning when the confirmand pairs them with a saint to admire, adding that person's name to their own.

Why this sacrament is so beneficial to receive in one's teens is because each generation is unique but peer pressures come within different groups. With the issues of your generation in mind, imagine one of teenagers today coupled not only in gender identity but their choices to have children. Learn from them. Endowed by their super virtues they talk to one other about how they will cope with an important issue of their day.

*At the Confirmation sponsors luncheon for their confirmands.*

"Five Confirmation parties rolled into one. I'm so excited" my neighbor's thirteen-year old daughter smiles deliciously, taking away the empty spoon of ice cream from her mouth.

"You should be. The party planner outdid herself. We'll have a teen band, a photo booth plus a photographer. Plus, I added face painters, party masks and favors. She planned a table game with prizes at the bottom of each guest's dinner plate. Don't tell anybody about that. I'm not good at keeping silly secrets," we laugh, happy to share in the plans for a super memorable day.

"This is a fun lunch, Aunt Laurel. Thank you," she says, as sweet as an angel.

"Here, here," I click my glass with a spoon and stand up from my chair around a table filled with nine other Confirmands and their Sponsors, each from our alt-group of childless women. "I propose a toast. To our beautiful, and handsome teenagers on the threshold of their Confirmation and reception of the gifts of the Holy Spirit, may each of you use virtue to transcend your limitations and transform lives," I hear unexpected Amens.

Rosa is next to hold up her glass. "A toast to the saints, whose lives inspire you and whom you honor. Shall we do a quick review? I know most of your saint's names. Jimmy yours is St. Joseph, the patron for fathers, a great choice. Julia yours is St. Joan of Arc, am I correct?"

"It was. I changed it to St. Nicholas. I want to be a pediatrician and he's the patron saint for children. I have time to change it back," she has a typical identity crisis.

Rosa focuses on another child, "Ginny, yours is? Don't tell me. Yours is St. Thomas More. You want to be a lawyer," she receives an enthusiastic "yes" in agreement.

"Billy, I remember yours, St. Joseph of Cupertino because you want to be a pilot. I had to research him. He is in the category of saints who levitate and bilocate. Very mysterious people," she exaggerates and he blushes. "And you my dear, Lily" she addresses her niece, "your saint is the Blessed Virgin Mary, herself."

"I want to have one son," she says waving an index finger in the air.

"If that's your plan, who will be your spouse?" Jimmy, the chaste namesake St. Joseph, wants to know.

"On your own? Whose surname would he have?" Ginny,

the inquiring would-be attorney, wants to know.

"Are you being serious or kidding?" Julia, the worried aspiring pediatrician, wants to know.

"Both," Lily shrugs.

"Oh, you mean like here and there," Billy, the every-where and -place saint, chuckles with an interesting answer.

The adults sit back and sharpen their wit for the teenagers' conversation ahead.

"There are a lot of ways to have babies. The regular mommy and daddy way," she looks to her Aunt Rosa for approval and gets an okay nod. "The in vitro way, the crispr way, the surrogate way, the egg harvesting way, the sperm bank way."

"Whoa," her aunt interrupts.

"I hear you. We understand," Deanna calmly glances around the table. "You don't have to be confused though. You have a right to knowledge about scientific methods. But let us ask you, if you emulate these saints as you say, and they were here to chat with you at this table, what might they say in response to your alt-choices to have children?"

"St. Nicholas would say, 'Ho, Ho, Ho-ly Cow!' There goes Christmas. No gifts, no decorations, cancel the holiday," Julia mimics and gets a round of laughs.

Following suit, Ginny says, "Let me see, I believe there is a canon law about surrogates, and oh yes, one on in vitro, and I believe we definitely have strong rules regarding sperm bank donations. Not to be confused with monetary bank donations."

"Ah, let me go next?" Billy, as St. Joseph of Cupertino, asks and is waved on. "We could have one baby with two bi-located fathers to a virgin mother at the same time. We could use donor sperm in a surrogate mother adopted by a married couple."

"Wait. Please?" Jimmy asks in his role play of St. Joseph. "I have to break my silence. All life is from God. I might only be in the seventh grade and thirteen-years old, but I know where we would be headed with birth conceived randomly. St. Joseph would be the most popular father around, because he would be everybody's foster father."

When the laughter dies down, both age groups understand how different the span of two generations are from each other and the issues at stake.

"Those are remarkable insights your saints have given you. If they were alive today, they might give the exact answers you gave. So, Lily, what do you say?" Laurel asks, palm extended for the final decision.

"I want one son," Lily still insists.

"Don't all children belong to you, Mother Mary?" Jimmy aka St. Joseph her husband wants to know.

Lily thinks and answers, "Through our son."

"Excuse me, are we ready to order," the waiter comes over to ask us.

---

## A Confirmation party of 300.

To accommodate the catering hall at Ildorato's, the party for the five confirmed children, their families and friends,

# The Body and Blood

have to be kept down to sixty in total for each. By 2:30 on Confirmation Sunday, the place is filled to capacity and rocking. The band is blasting, young- and middle- ages are out on the dance floor. The surrounding dinner tables are filled with cheerful older guests whose plates are covered with an array of scrumptious appetizers from the buffet. Each of the five sponsors is seated at our confirmand's table but join up for a quick rehearsal in the anteroom before a remarkable after dinner show.

"Here, let's go for one more practice," Sophie pulls Ava's sleeve and the three of us follow. Reassembled, "Rosa, start us off in the right key."

Doing so, she directs us to stand in our ordered places, and then takes out a tiny harmonica from her handbag. She breathes a D note and counts one, two, three with her fingers in the air, on cue we begin together upbeat but at a slower tempo than The Doobie Brothers rock group.

"Jesus is just alright with me, Jesus is just alright, oh yeah. I don't care what they may say. I don't care what they may do. Jesus is just alright, oh yeah," and that is where we stop, because more than a half-dozen nosey guests enter the room to watch us. Rosa wants the performance to be a surprise, and shoos everyone out of the room.

During dessert, we perform to the delight of everyone and inspired, one of us says that our friend's mother is celebrating her 90th birthday in a different room and we should sing for them too. In a small community, word gets around and our popularity is fun for a while. Putting a smile on people's faces and a song in their heart, this makes a lasting impression. Those who sing pray twice. Among ourselves, we laugh recalling our one-time-only show and our neighbors' reaction to us for weeks later.

There were other performers that day, a cousin of Claire's confirmand's family sang the Ave Maria in a bel canto voice that made everyone cry or think of crying, a professional dance couple, relatives of Ava, wowed us with an energetic cha-cha to a Four Seasons hit, and face painters delighted us, drawing whimsical expressions on some of the young.

*There is another recollection from this party, that produced the opposite feelings.*

Walking through the large lounge that connects the dining room with the restrooms, a man older than me called for my attention. At first remarkable for his reddish-brown cashmere suit that distracted from his overweight frame, he says that I look familiar. Immediately, he places me in a few activities I was involved with in the neighborhood years back. He explains that he is waiting for his son and asks if I do not mind reminiscing about the good old days. He says that he moved from the neighborhood over twenty years ago and mentions several people from that time who I knew and are still active in the community. He seems to know them very well and before I realize it we have been talking for 15-minutes. Suddenly, I catch myself and wonder aloud where his son is. His answer is vague and I feel our meeting might be a flirtation. I become uncomfortable and leave. Reentering the dining room, Ava stands akimbo with a look to match.

"Who were you talking to?"

"Why so fresh? He's a guest."

"What did he talk about?"

"Ava, why are you so upset? Before I say another word, you have to say."

"Come over here. People are listening," she pulls my

sleeve and I move to where she wants. "Do you know who he is?"

I gesture that I haven't a clue.

"He, he's Mafia," her voice is almost inaudible. "Not just any wise guy. He's the head of a family."

"Really?" I don't know what to do with the information. She smacks the side of her head.

"Aren't you the one, who thinks your stepfather was knocked off?"

"Shh! What are you saying? You go too far, Ava."

"Well?"

"Who is he? He said that he was waiting for his son, but he never came. We were talking for a long time. I started to feel awkward," I whisper frantically.

"He's a Don."

"So he's a Don. What is that to me?"

"He would know. That's what it means to you."

"What do you want me to do? Go back over and say, Mr. Don, do you know who might have kidnapped and killed my stepfather?" With these words out, I have to catch my breath. "Ava, if they scare you, you can imagine how I feel. If they are involved and they know you're my friend and we talk, you should be scared too."

"I'm not scared. I have nothing to do with them. They're cafone."

"I may look all Irish, but I'm half Italian and raised by

them. I'm not on guard when talking to one, but the Mafia. Drop it," I command, taking her by the hand and leading her back into the mainstream of the room.

"You should know his name. It's Stefano."

I'm frozen in place. Stefano is the surname on the Christmas cards.

At that moment, Father Leonardi is walking past us, observes our concerned look, but becomes distracted by another parishioner.

---

*You can't force any vocation. Let go and let God.*

"Father Mike," a member of the Holy Name, Mr. Odorisio, calls out walking quickly towards me. "Father, I saw them go up to the third floor. Don't look for trouble, but stop them," he says menacingly and adds, "Good luck. Catch them before they do it."

He takes my hand and enfolds it in his as if in a common prayer. "Act first, pray later," I pull away and take the staircase to run up the two flights. In a minute, I am facing the ballroom door. In the absence of a party, I take heed and resist my impulse to burst into the room. The husband of the couple who I have been courting to allow their son to try a vocation, is supposedly in there committing adultery. Quietly, I open the door and enter. I am accosted by the sounds of lovemaking. I assume I am too late and slam the door as I exit.

"Too hell with this. My God, why have you done this to me?" I hit my hand on the wall. "This was a good man. I pushed him too hard for his son. He wasn't ready to give him up for you. This sin is on me," my anger wells up. I control it and drop to my knees wrapping my arms around my chest, my heart is broken for this couple. "Please, Father, let me save their marriage? I beg you." Behind the door, there is laughter. Quickly, I stand. The door opens. They are two teenagers who exit, not the man I had thought.

They run sheepishly past me. My heart still pounding, I enter the room to catch my breath. The sound of lovemaking persists. Apparently, Mr. O and I were thinking about different couples and misinterpreted each other as to whom we each had in mind up here. I am past the shock and anger, and more disappointed over the situation of the lovers' hideaway at the Confirmation party. I kick a chair with meaning. Their sounds stop. I wait.

Disheveled, Gene Lustig and a woman looking half his age emerges. Without an exchange of words or emotional grimace, I leave. Infidelity aside, only marriage puts sex in a proper context for me. If I craved his type of a thrill, I would go parachuting. He'll turn up in confession with the same old, same old. I mistook his repentance at the hospital as his epiphany. His reform is typical for most, a cycle of relapses.

# 7

# Three Tests of Fortitude

*Father Mike leads by his good example for friends.*

"Smell the ocean air?" is the greeting Gene greets me with as I get into his silver Ford Transit, the van we use to go back and forth to the shelter and for similar charity work.

"What is that? Your latest air freshener to camouflage my smoking?" I take a deep breath.

"You like it?"

"I'll take the solution of an air freshener to satisfy people's reserve around me rather than a chastity belt to solve your issues," I intend to make my point as often as I can until he confesses and means it.

"I would like it better if you didn't smoke, and you would like me if I were married or celibate. Let's see who reforms first."

"You really equate us on that basis? I'm an ordained Catholic priest. You're 60 years old and still have hopes to start a family with a woman in her 20s? Romance not seduction, maximize your commonality with the future Mrs. L. How about starting with a 45-year old?"

"Second timers?" he snaps back.

"Maybe someone with a child, a son, you can help raise. Would that be so bad?"

"I date women with children. Too many issues. I'm a Godfather. That's enough."

"Not really. Life is personal or public. True, your personal life is your own, but if you hang with me, you have to clean up your image. Religion is a different ball game, do you agree?" I want his answer.

"Believe it or not, I'm trying."

"You'll get there," I am ready to drop the topic.

"To Lake Shore and beyond," he is ready to shift into drive as I buckle up.

"We're not going via Lake Shore today. We're going to a shelter in Cicero," I'm nonchalant about the change.

"Where exactly?"

"Lawndale. A shelter for pregnant women. Ten miles over the bridge. Let's go. I have a 10:30 appointment with the Sister who runs the home," I explain briefly.

"Your call," he puts the name into the GPS and we are on our way.

Gene has become my sidekick on these missions. He's old enough to be my dad. Since the death of Marco, he is finding his way, so I lead. Regarding women, his judgment is skewed. I see him as vain. He sees me as someone to keep him busy. When we arrive at the shelter, the extern nun escorts me into the sitting room and then takes Gene to the kitchen for coffee where he stays and reads his newspaper. In no time, the Mother Superior appears.

"Father Leonardi, we finally meet" says the woman dressed in her stalwart white habit of the Missionary of Charity.

# The Body and Blood

In the realm of the religious, our meeting pre-approved by the Bishop is blessed.

"Sister Mariam, this is an honor." She invites me to sit with her at a small pedestal table with two facing side chairs below a picture of her foundress, Mother Teresa with Pope John Paul II, both canonized saints.

"The Bishop's secretary informed me very little about the purpose of your visit Father, other than you come to offer us help with our families here."

She is honest and soft-spoken. I put down my guard. "May I be plain with you, Sister?" she gives the nod I expect. "I have been courting parents in my parish with sons and daughters who may have vocations, too zealously. I am here to seek such potential among the poorest of families you support."

"Oh, dear Father I have been waiting for such favor. In the seven years we have carried out our ministry, several families have struck us as devotees. Without additional support for them, other than to help a mother through her pregnancy, our dream for their future ends. Occasionally, an infant will be baptized and watched over by Godparents from the men and women who are our benefactors. This is a holy joy for us, but all the others we lose," with remorse she bows her head. "Do you truly have a way to change that, Father?"

She is a sister I would move heaven and earth for, but we share the same mountain to climb. Except, for me at this time, I am doomed if I fail to try. "Let me start with two families, and I will provide for all their needs," before I finish, she interrupts.

"They have too many, Father. They include basic necessities plus acceptance. Can you imagine such a circle of friends who will think well of them and not as broken and homeless?"

"My Sister, Joseph fled with Mary and Jesus to Egypt for refuge. Once, they were immigrants. I will provide your families with housing, employment, education, and ministries at a local church. What I ask of you is to choose them, two if there are such pious people among you. Not a tribe," I see the glee in her eyes. "A family, parents and their children," I take out my wallet and remove a card with my contact information. "Call, email, visit my parish, use a carrier pigeon," I have caught her off guard. She reveals her enthusiasm, reaching out for my card with a hint of giddiness but also with solemn gratitude.

Ending my first visit on this note, Gene and I make the short trip back, which is one of many during the process of meeting prospective families. I have asked this favor of Sister for two reasons. One, it is my penance. Beside myself in anger, that I might have sparked the temptation of a family man to commit adultery as an option to influence his son as the perfect person to fill my shoes in the priesthood, my confessor through the inspiration of the Holy Spirit directed me to seek vocations in another way. Second, leading by the example of Jesus Christ to do the will of the Father, my prayer and hope is Gene will prioritize family love much above eros and when he does, as a trusted friend of mine, I will share with him two families of this ministry of the Sisters and mine to foster. My cigarette smoking has nothing to do with his resistance.

---

*A faithfully departing parishioner leads by his example of trust in God and love to his wife, family, and friends.*

The sacrifice of the Mass is exactly that, a perpetual sacrifice of the body of Christ renewed for the redemption of the world to come. How do we know this? We wait, however long or brief we live until God unites us in that mystical body. I am one of thousands of parishioners in my parish. Yet, when a loved one, a friend, dies it feels as if there is only a small group of us. This is my account of a treasured friend's husband, who recently passed and my meager insight into the greatness of his holy character.

Rosa's husband died. Paul was 62 and retired less than a year. Among her reflections of him was that he was so young. Indeed, his type of death makes everyone feel let down. When the average man or woman, who is busy at work their whole life, either right before or soon after their retirement dies, people are disappointed. There ought to be a few years off to celebrate the completion of a job well done. God rested. When his work was accomplished, He scheduled it on a day called the Sabbath, which is literally one-seventh of time. Upon our retirement, my mom and I shopped, made a local pilgrimage, threw birthday parties and went to them plus ate out with friends more than at home. Other folks go on exciting foreign trips, start a new hobby, buy the car of their dreams, visit family and friends more, spend time in their retirement home away from home. With so many doctor appointments, Paul and Rosa didn't get to do much of that at all.

Until the super flood hit our neighborhood, Paul and Rosa were just a couple we saw at Sunday Mass or at a church social. But when both our houses here flooded and our area lost heat and electricity, we were rescued separately and together by a mutual friend, Claire. We stayed at her hi-rise apartment with four more parish acquaintances for three straight weeks. Getting to know Paul, we discovered that he was a silver-lining type person. When at dinner praying *Grace Before Meals* and going around the table to express our gratitude, Paul would say how the disastrous experience was for him "bitter sweet." I remember that because this was the best way to think through our ordeal.

Paul is the President of the parish Holy Name Society and reminds me of my stepfather in that way, because Frank was the Treasurer for a while. In another way, both men were previously married. Although with different types of endings to their marriages, their second marriages are also in the Church with proper annulments in order. A little unusual for couples in a Catholic community to be identified as such, so it is encouraging to recognize not just their acceptance but their leadership positions.

Like Frank, Paul is the silent presence in a group of women. At a breakfast or luncheon where he was usually the only male, Paul sat quiet, content to listen. "Paul, what do you think?" Rosa would ask, and Paul would give his opinion. Rosa absorbed his every word and repeated them here and there in her own words. They are a loving couple, who pray in earnest that he be cured of his illness. Our alt-group of women pray. The Third Order Franciscans, of whom he is a member, pray. The Sisters of Mother Teresa and other prayer groups invoke prayers for his healing. Close friends, family members pray the most. On the night he passes-on, Rosa, Claire, Sophie, and I are at his bedside. Paul's last words to his wife are, "I love you."

People die in all sorts of ways. The cruelest death is of a young child. They have no mind that is cognizant of life's potential. When God takes one home, their void is filled with the joy that their nine-month arrival brought and then, the sorrow left in their leaving too soon commences. The bravest deaths are the heroes and heroines who accept their destiny in service to a grateful God, family, and country. The worst ways to die are against the free will of any person who is out of line with the will of God. Paul put up a good fight and breathed his last breath in the whispers and tears of passionate prayers. Before his interview into heaven along with a resume of a life well spent, his soul is heaven bound.

Nevertheless, grief is devastating. So much so, I sometimes wish that the memories of our loved ones would leave with them, but how would we experience art and prayer? So much energy is spent on loving those who have earned our love a thousand times over and are departed. Authors write books to treasure their life's story, artists capture their images in painting, composers write them in music, builders dedicate great edifices in their names. I guess that is what we do with the saints and angels. I think of the names of parish churches like that.

---

*Father John leads with his challenges and obedience to the Diocesan Bishop.*

The letter I received from the Bishop's office sending me for a psychological evaluation disappoints me, but the phone calls I receive from the parish friends I am separated from about the death of their loved ones saddens me more. In my priesthood, I have become persona non grata. I walk into a local church that has a sign outside that reads "Confessions today 3 to 4 PM." It doesn't matter that the priest isn't my Spiritual Director. My soul thirsts for salvation.

"Bless me Father for I have sinned, I am a priest involved in a non-sexual query and in need of a confession. I am discouraged in my faith. Every day, my loyal friends from the parish that I have been removed from sustain me with tweets, emails, and Facebook messages which the Bishop forbids me to reply, and I comply. I miss their celebrations, overlook their comfort in my friendship, but my absence from the wakes and funerals of them is too much to bear. The loved ones they lost, I also loved."

"This is harsh. What is the distinction Christ made between the letter and spirit of the law?" he asks.

"I will send a Mass card," I'm depleted and too emotionally spent to say more.

"We take a vow of obedience to our Bishop and I cannot speak for him. I can speak the words of Our Lord and absolve you by his authority. However, coming for confession, you already passed both tests, the one to our God and to our Bishop, my brother."

# 8

# *Parish Stories that Overlap*

*Taking the pursuer seriously, Laurel seeks the advice of Father Mike.*

There is only one person who I can talk with about this, and it is not my mother. I cannot believe the boldness of this man. What does he think I will do? My mind is racing a hundred miles an hour. At the door of the rectory, I am buzzed in. Exchanging greetings, Donna says that the pastor is available to see me. Father is on the phone when I enter, and he waves me in, pointing to the chair in front of his desk. He is talking about a repair on the church property, which in a minute seems settled to his liking.

"Good to see you, Laurel. What's up?"

"I'm sorry to make an abrupt visit. I wouldn't unless I had to tell someone. He's stalking me. Frank's murderer," I can't express myself clearer. I feel numb.

"What do you mean? What happened? Who and where?"

"In the parking lot behind the supermarket. I was backing the car out of the spot slowly, because it's hard to see. No car was coming. My navigator would have gone off. Then, slam, bang. I backed right into the side door of a car driving behind me."

"Was anybody hurt?"

## The Body and Blood

"We're fine. The driver was an old man. He got out of the car and apologized. 'Sorry. I'm sorry. Are you alright?'," I hold my hand out to Father, indicating the man's same gesture. "He said it was his fault. He cursed himself. He looked over my car, saying he would pay. There wasn't a scratch on my car. His had a big dent in it. I was never in an accident where the other driver accepted one hundred percent of the blame. I was sort of speechless. He kept talking. I said a few words before the whole thing was over. He gave me his card 'if any damage is underneath somewhere,' he said," I place the man's card on the pastor's desk. He motions that he doesn't want it.

"Why do you think he's stalking you? It sounds like an ordinary fender bender."

"After the man drove away, I stood against my car for a moment. I hit him and he blamed himself. I looked up his address on my iPhone. It's a department store. I looked up his name. None of the images resembled his. I called. No such number. Bogus. I started to think about how the whole accident happened. I was so careful, his insistence on it being his fault. He pushed the card in my hand like he wanted me to know it was fake. Something familiar about his face. He was dressed so differently, so out of context than the man I had met. His car was old, dirty, messy inside with papers and stuff. He looked sloppy. Except for his manner. His manner was polite. It was him, Father. I'm convinced."

"Who? Who is him?" he asks, trying to decode my alarm.

"The man at Ildorado's, at the Confirmation party. Ava told me he's a Don, the same name on the Christmas cards. Could he be the murderer of my stepfather?"

"Are you ready to go to the police?" he seems to ask a

115

logical question but my assessment is different.

"And say what? I received a couple of greeting cards from a mobster, who I think wants me to know about my stepfather's disappearance 25 years ago and because I left it at that, he is stalking me? The same person in the car accident with me in a parking lot, with no damages and no witnesses. Not doing it. But, I do want a reliable person to help me figure out what it is he wants."

"Realistically, you're trying to get in the mind of a psychotic? I think it's the other way around. Apparently, he wants to get into your thoughts."

"I do feel that I am the one pursued. Tell me, please. What does he want from me?"

"Laurel, you're asking me to think like a sick man. A man who you believe confesses his murders to a priest, and then receives the Eucharist from you and your mother for his gratification. Since he no longer lives in the parish community, no priest in residence here is likely to have given him absolution, and if one did the penance might have been why he moved."

My thoughts are calm. He has given me a satisfactory explanation of why this man no longer lives in the neighborhood, and an open-ended question as to whether he went to confession to a priest I knew back then.

"Laurel, you're an intelligent woman. If I thought you would discard my advice, I would not give it. Monsignor Luke and all the priests before him helped you through your life's trials. I will also."

"I deliberately signed up for theology classes, because I was at a loss to understand my environment. I love Mass and

# The Body and Blood

Communion. Is that why this is happening to me?"

"I don't know. How is school helping you make the connections anyway?"

"I believe it is bringing my questions to the surface. Thinking about the dynamics in a parish community is not unlike any environment, but from a religious perspective it is night and day."

He is silent. I feel that Father wants me to share my insight. Of the two, I am less afraid of the questions than the answers.

"Go ahead, tell me."

"Why do friends go to confession behind their friends back, rather than just talk to the person? How does a priest, who comes to help us in America because of a shortage, become entangled in unproven accusations for years and shunned? Where else but in church could a murderer, who is unbeknown to the women whose husband and stepfather he has killed, walk freely and receive from them the Host of God?

"Any answers?"

"Revelations. Those are certainly not questions Christ shied away from. He was betrayed and denied by friends, rebuffed falsely but stood his ground, and mocked for his spirit and authority."

"Laurel, I will be here to encourage you in your faith. I advise you to talk with your professors, they will narrow your concerns and help you define what discipline and topic will give you greater understanding. But, they are hornets' nests you have stirred up. Add a rosary to your daily prayers for a week," he advises. "Please, take the card," he points to it still on his desk.

"If not for being pursued, these questions would be dormant. But he won't stop," I say and take out a tissue and pick up the card placing it carefully in an empty envelope he has on the desk and say, "fingerprints." Adding what is in my heart, "I am in this alone, but in your company" adding softly "God be with you."

"And also with you," I hear his prayerful response.

I leave behind my timid feelings and go with the strength I feel empowered by.

---

*Father Mike reflects on how the separate lives of parishioners with their parish priest can converge.*

There are many types of relationships in which we can safely transfer our negative feelings into positive ones. Some include our parents, certain family members spouses, siblings, our friends, as well as professionals. Among men and women in government, healing, and educational careers, they are usually given titles added to their names. Often they will wear a uniform, distinct clothing, to identify their occupation. An example is that I wear clerics and am called Father. Seminarians are well-educated on this psychological phenomenon. There are codes of ethics in virtually all careers. In my religious vocation, this is one of the reasons for celibacy and obedience and for order priests the inclusion of their poverty. The claim that Laurel makes of the duplicity of a parishioner harassing her is also troublesome to me. I am aware of evil and the sins committed in my parish. While my involvement with all of my members is on a priestly level, hers and her mother's is both religious and personal as women ministers of the Word and the Eucharist and as a wife and a stepdaughter who are no more.

*For now, I must be off to Louis's sister's wedding. He is my interested seminarian.*

The risk of catering a reception for a hundred people in one's backyard under an event tent pays off when the weather turns out as ideal as this June day. With a light breeze and mild temperature, the fresh outdoor air after a typical snowed in Chicago winter feels inspiring. The band is not overly loud, the waiters less conspicuous, the dance floor off to the side brings the festivity inward where feelings are comfortable and homey.

Out on the dance floor for a waltz, a man taps my shoulder. "Father Leonardi, I am Louis' grandfather, Jim Stefano."

Making his acquaintance, in an instance I recognize his dance partner as my old college classmate. "Susan!"

"Mike," she smiles back.

"This is a surprise. Let's switch, shall we?" says Mr. Stefano, who holds out his hand to my parishioner, who glances at me, and then accepts with the two gliding off.

"I heard you were a priest," Susan says big eyed as we take smaller steps.

"Really? You don't think I fit the clerics, well," I tug at my Roman collar.

"I thought of becoming a nun."

"But?"

"Nothing, I still might."

# The Body and Blood

"Interesting. Why?"

"I'm single, 42, and have dated two boys my whole life!"

"Boys or men?"

"Is that a trick question, Mike?" she gives a smirk.

I avoid answering, give her a twirl, and we dance until the joyful rhythm of the song ends.

"That was so much fun. You are as sweet as I remember you. Nice to see you," she says letting go about to leave.

"Wait, you have to tell me more about why you want to be a nun. We need real ones," a thought that stops her.

"Real ones? Oh, I know. You have a group of church women who don't see you as a dozen cloistered nuns but with a personality."

"I'm holy but yes, my ministry is in a large parish. I roll with their feedback. That doesn't lessen how I would like to add programs particularly for our seniors. Simply put, I lack the people resources nuns or sisters would provide."

"Sounds admirable. The truth is I've tried, Mike. Two Mother Superiors passed on my request. I'm an assistant principal, vested in my benefits. I could join an order and not be a burden. But even with brothers and sisters, I'm the only single one. I take care of my parents who have come to depend on me."

"How old are they?"

"My parents are in their 80s. My responsibilities come first. I'm happy. I just don't like to dwell on what I don't have and count the blessings I do. The school children I work around have that effect on me. I have a long way to retire. I'm in a good parish, and am one of those do-gooders you love," she puts her hands together in a sweet prayerful pose.

"Um, you're well-trained, Susan. What parish?"

"St. Ann's, where the wedding was held today."

"The pastor's Father Murray. I'll be asking him about you."

"We'll keep in touch through him," she says, ready to walk away, then turns to give me one of those smiles, "Mike Leonardi, a priest. Yeah, I get it."

Her sacrifice is the most familiar to me: it is what she has in common with my 9 o'clock attendees. The favorite child, Jacob's Joseph, the siblings leave behind only to wind up caring for their parents and exalting others in their good deeds.

"Father Leonardi, there you are," someone calls me and my time is reconnected elsewhere in a nanosecond.

"Father, come to the table, they're taking our orders," Roy, one of the brothers of the bride, comes over and I follow him back to our table. "Here's your seat, Father. This is Joe to your left and Ken on your right. I'll wave to you from the opposite side," he says pointing to his empty seat at the table across from us and leaves.

Meanwhile, an open hand comes across my chest to greet me. "Hi, I'm Joe Andolini, an honor to meet you, Father." Followed by the hand from my right side, "I'm Ken Tommasino, good to be with you, Father."

Without realizing it, my reaction is off guard, "Those are two characters in the Godfather," their laugh makes me uncomfortable. I avoid their conversation and instead of enjoying the novelty of meeting new people, I talk directly to familiar faces at my table. However, it seems obvious to me that Stefano, that plotter who just happened to be dancing with an old schoolmate of mine and seats me between these goodfellas, wants to catch my attention. He is either discouraged or possibly encouraged that Louis has talked with me about the priesthood.

Joe and Ken are up and about allowing me to leave them unnoticed. Never would I have anticipated going from the frying pan into the fire.

"Father Leonardi," a much older and taller man than I, appears in the narrow pathway en route to a friend.

"Yes, and the pleasure of whom?"

"Manny Capone. My friends call me Manny."

"As in Al Capone?" I exaggerate his alias.

"Living in Chicago, I get that a lot. I imagine 'Father' is what all people hear when they first meet you."

His words are distinct and voice louder than the average person's. I am direct, "Is this meeting by chance or does it have a purpose?"

"Just casual. I wanted to compliment you on the renovations in your church. The marble work is especially beautiful," he says in perfect English but comes across as gangster to my ears.

"We worked hard to get it right."

"I used to live in the parish about thirty-years ago before we moved out to the burbs. You have the same pretty Eucharist people as back then. I even received Communion from one, but she didn't recognize me. What are they women priests?"

"Hardly. Manny, say what you want to or step out of my way," I smile, but my voice reveals my emotion, as does his.

He leans over so that I can only hear him and says, "She and her mother have no right on the altar. We did away with their old man. The mom is too old to bother with, but the daughter is still a useful scapegoat."

"She's knows all about how you project your sins onto her in your vain confessions," pushing him out of my way. I feel his hand on my shoulder.

"You know how much I give to the Church?" His tone of voice is loud and angry. "You think you can survive on their pittance? I'm who I am. Don't tell me anyone is more generous and Catholic than me, especially a divorced woman who never had children. What is she except damaged?"

"You see this smile on my face?" I say pointing. "Beneath it is a mouth that will devour you from the pulpit. My people tithe freely, unlike you who give back what is stolen from others. You think the men and women in my church want to associate with a murderer, an adulterer who transmits disease? What commandment haven't you broken or beatitude underestimated? Sure, I'm ordained to absolve you from the sins you genuinely repent of, but God sees all and is still your judge. But, you Mr. Wise Guy murdered a righteous member of my Holy Name Society. You take away every good feeling people have about themselves and think your pittance will redeem you. Not in my heaven on earth. I'd rather convert the world than have you pray under my roof. Now, get out of my way."

"I don't have to change one bit. I offer the Church any

one of my children, and children's children. They'll redeem me. The woman is a wasteland," his voice is raised so that all the wedding guests stop to listen.

The argument is undefended. I am alone in its resonance with onlookers stunned. As I leave, I pass Louis and his parents who look at me understandingly.

Louis, the hopeful seminarian, follows me out to make apologizes and tells me the person's real name, Mr. Johnny Torrio. I recognize it from hearsay, as a Stefano hitman.

---

## *The status quo of the ousted Father John.*

A ping sound comes over the computer and the third of my eight brothers and sisters scheduled for the virtual chat appears.

"Hey, John. How are you? Hey, Karol. I miss you buddies," the youngest, Eric, appears on screen.

"I'm holding up. Karol has been giving me free advice," I try to be upbeat. Just seeing and hearing my brothers makes me feel happy and hopeful.

"Yeah, I told him to hire an attorney and sue them," Karol, the lawyer, half jokes.

"This is serious, isn't it? Your Bishop is involved. Were you really removed from your parish?" Eric is rightfully worried.

"What can I say? Yes and Yes. I tried to help. I befriended two parishioners who turned against me," I try to isolate the problem.

"Singles," Karol personifies.

"Aren't they old people?" Eric raises his voice. "Old single people caused the mess you're in? How is that possible?"

Another ping is overheard and a fourth party joins the virtual.

"I scheduled everybody a few minutes apart. Let me click on Stan," I say, activating his audio.

"John. This is Stan. Can you see me?"

"Click on facial connect," I raise my voice. He does and his big head appears peering into the screen.

"Hi, you guys. Good to see you all. How's my favorite brother," I'm not his favorite but at this moment, I appreciate the kindness.

"Holding up. Helpless though," I say adding a feeling I seldom have.

"Work with that, own it, but fight your way out. You're bigger than that," Stan commands me. He is a high school coach.

"As a priest, I am helpless. Not as a man. When Christ called himself a shepherd and his people sheep, he meant it. That's how they are being treated, but I am suddenly the wolf."

"How do you occupy your time? With five kids, we can't imagine solitude," Eric says, as if that is the worst outcome of my situation.

"Eric, I spend a lot of time praying. Especially for you and yours," I laugh him off. My other brothers get it. Eric slightly.

Another ping is overheard and a fifth party is on time to

join.

"Hannah," we each call out our sister's name. She is equally excited, and names us one by one. She is the psychologist in the family.

"How could this happen to you? You grew up with Mama and Papa. You know old people, baby brother."

"I do."

"He does. He's a priest though," Karol says.

He wants her to think about me in a role that defines my manhood and vulnerabilities differently.

"Hannah, it is not my name I am defending. I represent the Church, herself. The issue of the siblings sponsoring an aide and making a legal arrangement with their attorney is dismissed."

"Then, you are exonerated. I knew they would excuse you. You don't know the laws of America and you are certainly naïve about their culture," Karol gets the practical arguments out of the way.

Another ping is overheard and a sixth party, the oldest sibling, is waiting.

"Hello Clara," we greet her before she does us.

"Hello, everyone. You are a fine bunch of good looking people. How are you all?" She evokes the same response, eliciting a cacophony of answers only her ears can decipher. "And my innocent brother?"

"He's holding his own," Eric answers instead.

"Are you John?"

Using her professional voice, she insists I speak for myself.

"The isolation is challenging. I am in a house with much older priests who don't relate well. The Bishop suspended my duties to celebrate Mass and to hear confessions."

"You didn't tell us that. When did that happen? What does that imply," Stan has one of his kids hanging on his neck. My sister-in-law waves to us from the distance of the doorway, waiting to take the child back.

"It means just that. I received a call from the Bishop's office two days ago. The siblings wrote to him. The Church does not want any type of scandal on top of what they are dealing with."

"You have to keep a low profile," Karol agrees.

"I have been, but I'm a social person. I feel useless."

"Work with that feeling in your prayers. A lot of people feel useless, especially old single-type people. That's who you're up against. People afraid of dying with nobody who wants to take care of them, except a hospital," Stan pictures a usual ending.

"You're right, I guess."

Another ping is overheard and a seventh sibling, Lena, joins us.

"You are all on? You said 7 o'clock. Hi everyone," we wave back at Lena.

"I spaced us out," I said quickly. "You're the busiest, with what's going on in your life. How was the move?"

"The house is so big. I'll give you all a tour when we finish. We have two guest rooms, but Jan and I could make room for all of you. Fill me in. What's happening with my favorite, best brother."

She's happy and a unanimous reaction of chuckles follows.

"He's holding his own," Eric jumps in again.

I feel like my old self. These people are so predictable in their love for me.

"Okay. Anyone want to trade places with me?" Eric says to an echo of no responses.

"Your Chicago singles can move in with us," Lena says. "Hannah told me a little of what happened. It's not like they're wrong, but boy oh boy they have nerve to take down a priest over their problems. Anyone up for a visit to the Windy City?"

She is teasing, but a few of my brothers and sisters take up her offer in jest.

"You are good people. Thank you, thank you for your love. You picked up my spirit," I miss their companionship. No relationship surpasses them. Their joy makes celibacy bearable. "But, I keep trying to tell you. The issue about the aide and the attorney is resolved. The siblings have made another claim against me," I have their attention. "They say that I broke the Seal of Confession," their reaction is the same from the few people I have confided in, 'huh?' "They say I revealed the confessions of a few of their friends. I'm told they want my collar."

"What are they doing? Displacing their feelings over bad priests on good ones? Who are these Americans you left us to help? You are the meekest man I know," Lena defends me.

"I thought I was, but I tell you, if I were not a priest I would charge them with defamation of character."

"That," Hannah snickers. "That is called cancel culture. You're hurt because you won't do to them what they did to you. I know you. You probably went to confession and blamed yourself for their behavior?"

"She's right. I bet you did," Eric agrees.

"Tell us. Go ahead. You blame yourself. Can't you see that is what they count on. Oh John, John, you big beautiful man," Karol holds his head in his hands.

"I want to stay a priest. I came to America to help and I'm losing my vocation. I can't let this happen," I say, feeling that I am about to break down.

The last ping and eighth invited guest is heard. I click and our mother is virtual.

"John?" She tests to verify the audible is on. "John, my dear?"

"Yes, mama. Your sound is working."

"We can all hear you, mama," Clara calls out.

"I see all my dumplings. My beautiful and handsome children. Your mama misses you,"

"We miss you too, mama," we are unanimous in our reply.

"John, Papa and I have made up our minds. You are

coming home. We sent you a ticket. It's in your email. You are booked for a flight next Monday. Enough," she is firm.

I start to protest, but my siblings one by one cut me off with reasons why our parents are right. I want the love of my family. Their hugs and kisses. To hold my nieces and nephews. To love and be loved.

"I'm coming home, mama."

# 9

# *Priorities and Divine Plans*

*Father Mike, his Retreat Master, and spiritual books.*

Born and raised a Chicagoan, my favorite retreat house is run by the Jesuits Fathers in Barrington. I can afford the short drive of an hour and make reservations with my Retreat Master for a 3 night stay to return by Sunday night while a priest friend covers my weekend Masses. Truth is, I desperately need a break.

Once there and settled in, my good friend Father Philip greets me in his office filled with the bright daylight from his picture window of an 80-acre pastoral scene on which the house sits. "Shall we renew our faith, my friend."

"I lost track of God's will. I had to pause the commotion around me, Philip."

We sit facing one another closer to the window with nature's view rather than the interior room design.

"My feelings are unraveling. The confessions of my parishioners and the prayers of the Church for vocations, I am at an impasse in my thoughts and words. Thank God, my duties anchor me," I say why I have come and gratefully so. He is posed to listen. "My parish was not long ago filled with the Mafia, but this is common knowledge. If I may, let me set the background. The previous pastor's team accepted them in every way. They gained a false sense of confidence. Feeling invincible, they increased their crimes, exposed themselves to the government, who collected evidence and prosecuted. The majority were sentenced to prison or moved out or went into hiding. Others changed their names or took fresh starts as witnesses for the government. These men left behind young, innocent families who through their profits and insulation built up the parish and the neighborhood. Today, they are good, prayerful Catholic people. But the past has a way of catching up with us all. I am talking about their victims. Two of my Eucharistic Ministers, a wife and a stepdaughter of a man killed by a wise guy 25 years ago, who has since been made a Don, continue to be pursued."

"Why and how has this mystery become resurrected?" He infers my involvement.

"One of the Don's grandsons has come to me expressing his desire to be a priest. At the same time, the daughter of the victim has also come to me saying she and her mother are being harassed all of a sudden by a Mafia figure."

"The mystery of God at work," he says. "The righteous and the unrighteous, observed from above by the Father and the Son. This is a resurrection story. The righteous will win."

"I am guessing that the murderer was given absolution but then he deliberately received Communion from the dead man's wife and stepdaughter. To me, he's the scum of the earth, but," I shake my index finger in the air "his grandson wants to be a priest. The child of the son is still living in my parish after he moved. The conflict is this young man is under my direction to enter the seminary this semester," I pause hoping Father interrupts. He refrains. "Righteousness belongs to God. My Eucharistic Minister has been pursued with cards and personal veiled threats the past two years, which coincides with the young man's vocational interest. The murderer cannot get my minister out of his head. I want my people to have vocations, but I am terrorized at what cost," I notice his uncomfortable reaction and realize that my hands are clutched like fists to the arms of the chair. On the end table between us, there is a Bible and carafe of water. He pours me a glass.

"The diocese assigned me as one of several priests to minister to Catholic men and women in the police department. My followers there, along with my close circle of parish men, surround and protect me. She and her mother are retired, with no family, and are completely exposed to the biased judgments within. My Eucharistic Minister is also a lector and reflects on what happened from a scriptural, and religious viewpoint. She knows that whomever she distributes Communion to, the person is reconciled or sacrilegious. She understands fully, and I believe for the sake of the religion she would die to protect me, but I am already surrounded by militant people. She is in a circle of Catholic academics," I look at him man to man.

"How do you know that she knows all this?"

"I am her Spiritual Advisor," I say throwing my hands up.

"Can she go to the police?"

"We discussed that. She has circumstantial and real evidence. The case is 25 years old. My brother, you know the righteous are as firm as the ones who want to steal heaven. At first, she confided only in me, but silence weighs heavily on people's minds. She decided to study theology at her alma mater, DePaul. Now, she talks with her professors and classmates, and writes papers on these topics. There is a passion about her. It won't be long until she writes a book to unburden what she knows. The Holy Spirit is active and alive."

"There is the other side: the mother who prays for her

son to be a priest. She knows her father-in-law is the head of her husband's family. She wants her son's freedom. This grandfather mocks us and our ministers by believing he can kill a righteous member of the Holy Name Society and be redeemed without atonement by fostering his grandson's priestly vocation. He uses confession as a means to justify his ends through religion. In truth, he has. Without me asking, his hitman confessed the murder and this scheme to me at a wedding the other day. The reason for my retreat."

"And Louis' father?"

"That is an answer and past I have yet to establish."

"Does the grandson know all this?"

"That his grandfather is a Don, he must, but of this crime no, I don't believe so. The young man honors his parents and his mother obeys her husband, that's all I can say."

"And your Eucharistic Minister talks openly with you about this?"

"The daughter's mother is sick and misspoke that at the time the police protected them. Many people in the parish, I suspect did. It wasn't until the murderer started to pursue them that the past became alive again. They received his second year's Christmas card and then, at a Confirmation party, he spoke with Laurel. A friend revealed his identity and name, it was the same. By then, Laurel etched his face in her mind, so that months later despite a disguise when he had a car accident with her, she recognized him and came to me in confidence. Her stepfather's blood cries out to this man and no amount of confessions can stop the sound without contrition. He has undone himself."

"And Laurel?"

## The Body and Blood

He wants me to own her side. "When the Church first started this ministry, they were asked to join. While both did so for a love of God and neighbor, after the disappearance of her husband, the mother acted more out of love for her daughter knowing she likely gave the murderer or accomplices Communion. Until now, Laurel was shielded but still knows she cannot prevent the will of God. These are gentle women. I doubt if anyone imagined this ministry could leave our women so vulnerable."

"I have no experience on how to resolve this problem," my Retreat Master is honest. "On the one hand, there is a young man who is the grandson of the man who killed your minister's husband and stepfather decades before you came on the scene. If he pursues the seminary, he must have a letter of recommendation from you. On the other hand, you are a Spiritual Advisor to your minister, whose stepfather you know is indirectly linked through this crime to the young seminarian to whom you are also an Advisor."

"Correct. Her question is in general and particular. At what cost does the Church expect their lay ministers to carry out their assistance to priests?"

"I see your dilemma, but the mind of God also imagines your solution. In the narrow sense you pastor a congregation, not one murderer, not one promising vocation, not one loving mother and daughter. In the broad sense your parish of thousands strong is part of the entire body of the universal Catholic Church. There is always an answer. You have come here to think of one of many that the Holy Spirit has designed for you. In the next two days, let us pray that you discern the spirit, so that all these souls are saved."

He blesses me and asks me to re-read a book I first encountered while in the seminary *The Cloud of Unknowing*.

The following afternoon, I talk about how the subject matter allows me to clarify my thoughts on the situation.

"An anonymous writer. Think of that, no credit but I have assigned the book to retreatants for the past 45-some years."

"I am thinking about my problem from too narrow a perspective. To start, let's sort out who knows who and the overall dilemma. The daughter and the murderer are fully aware of what is going on and of each other. Her mother knows the what but not the who. The grandson wasn't born at the time and is innocent of the crimes of his grandfather but that he is a criminal, he knows. The mother, wife of the murdered husband, was deliberately kept out by the detectives, if for no other reason than to protect her and her daughter. There was no body, no witnesses, so no crime, for their record he remains an 80-year-old missing person.

The dilemma is the bigger picture. Why the murderer is obsessed with the victims seems easier to understand than not. Both women are among the first to have ministries within the sanctuary. They were in the public eye in- and out- side of Church. The mother was insulated by the corporate authority of her franchise, and her agents couldn't make the deals their goodfellas wanted. With the daughter's guardians at school and work, the husband alone was vulnerable. The Mafia are men who refuse to look weak regardless of who says no to them, but women? Not a chance. He was clearly their target."

"Feasible. It was the '80 and '90. The Church did expect a reaction to women in our exclusive roles. Plus, it isn't hard to imagine him being envious of the wife's business and ashamed of her daughter's knowledge of them. So where are we Mike?"

Again, he wants me to own her story. I'm succinct: "The

Mafia."

"You said that she is protected by her environment. The daughter and mother have longevity in the parish and friendships with parishioners, neighbors, fellow ministers, and a valued work reputation. You are underestimating their circles of contacts. The Mafia's relatives who stayed in the parish either don't know or forgot about the murder, nor do they want much to do with the criminal side of their families. If you believe that the women are being sacrificed, they will triumph in the name of Christ. You are the pastor of His church and only He remains the true sacrifice and victor."

"I can't see a way out for her."

"What is the way you see that is not 'the way' out? This is happening among your parishioners. Her inquiry goes to doctrine. She wants to know why she and her mother were and are expected to be the Extraordinary Ministers of the Eucharist to the man or men involved in killing her stepfather and her mother's husband."

"Give me another book. Maybe that will help me?"

"John of the Cross."

"I haven't read him either since the seminary."

"Read it."

Before opening the book, I press the *Dark Night of the Soul* between my hands in prayer, "God Almighty, I do believe. Help my unbelief."

On the third day with Philip, he hears my confession: "Bless me Father for I have sinned. I am selfish with my problems. If not for this retreat, I would be left in the darkness of my dilemma. My priority is the young man who has a vocation. I will pray for a way to share with him knowledge of his grandfather's past crimes and ways he secretly continues to harm these women and perhaps others, the very parishioners who helped inspire his love for the priesthood. It's a lesson he might benefit from for himself one day. If his vocation is true, he will find his own way to stop his grandfather from his ill-intentions."

"If he can, and if he can't? What about your mother and daughter ministers?"

"He will rise to the challenge. I have faith."

"You are asking a young man who has yet to commit to enter the seminary to be dependent on your faith. He must have his own virtue to handle his grandfather. What if he can't, and your plan for him falls apart. What about the women?"

"You said it yourself. Don't underestimate their layers of associations. They may be alone, but they are very visible in their public and private communications. I can encourage them in these resources, but I can only do so much. I am a pastor of thousands."

"Three days is a short time to solve the problem of the Mafia," my advisor empathizes. "Did you know St. Teresa of Avila inspired John of the Cross and that her book, *Interior Castle*, was written before his? It's rhetorical. Women are more resilient than men realize. That's your final penance, Mike. Your faith is remarkable, never doubt that. You came this distance out of your concern not for yourself but a few of your sheep. You will work this out one way or another. Your problem is in the hands of God."

Father Philip and I part until the next time.

Back at my parish after three days on retreat, I am the celebrant that Monday at the 9, and I am renewed with a treasure trove of ideas.

---

*Laurel and her mother.*

Again, the aides tell me that the obsession my mother has over the missing body of her husband has resurfaced. As much as I want to separate those thoughts from mine, I cannot, given the cards and coincidences from the one man who personifies such a murderous deed. Hers is a topic I approach delicately.

"That was an interesting movie," I begin, having selected a plotline that was an appropriate segue for our discussion. "The more I watch it, the more I see hidden messages in it for us. Am I right?"

"Maybe. Laurel, hand me the dessert dish please," she avoids the opportunity to chat.

"I'm glad your appetite is normal. It makes it easy for me to cook for us. Is the cake good?"

"Very good. Mother doesn't mean to be short with you. My memory makes it difficult to talk sometimes and frustrating."

Picking up on a word, I take a deep breath and begin. "Frank's memory was a little off before he disappeared, wasn't it?"

"Yes, but he was healthy and knew to stay close to home."

"He knew all the names of his grandchildren and great-grandchildren, didn't he?"

"Yes, he was a family man. He kept us all in mind," she says again in an assertive tone.

"Mother, your aides have mentioned that you are talking about Frank and are upset that he hasn't been found."

"He can't be found. He's dead. They killed him."

"Do you want to talk about it? I do," I reach over to hold her hand.

"Frank was killed. What more is there to say."

"Did the police hold back information from you?"

"No. There was no body. They saw I had a business to run. You were working. We had a lot of community support. Why do you want to talk about this?"

"Nothing. Your aides said it was on your mind."

"Maybe. Maybe, I'm worried that it hasn't been resolved and I won't be here to protect you. It is on my mind," she slowly discloses her upmost feelings.

"So you think there is a reason the killer still wants to hurt us?"

"We don't have the business anymore. I shouldn't be worried, but I am. I love you very much."

"There was rampant crime in the neighborhood back then. Is that how the police saw it?"

"More or less. It's over. I just have this mother's intuition about something. Are you alright? Why are you talking about this?"

"I told you. Your aides say that it is on your mind

lately."

"Okay, we'll end the conversation. Whenever God takes me, I want you to stay close to the parish and to DePaul. You need the support of both communities, not one without the other. You talk, and you write," she sighs but with a smile. "You can't control that. I don't want you to. I do want you to be careful. I want you to pray."

"Oh, God. That is the best advice you can give me."

My mother and I were always in sync. While it was challenging to let her go a year from then, I came to respect and to believe more and more in the spiritual gift of a mother's intuition.

She was right. With the case of Frank's missing body still open and us living in the same neighborhood, it would be imprudent for me to rely solely on the circle of people in my parish. That I had another group of religious people at DePaul gave me the balance I needed to keep my faith strong and vibrant. Locally, I was vulnerable. I did not have the same image at my alma mater. My self-awareness with who I am posed no threat to anyone, except what they made up in their own minds. As a psychologist, I practiced control over my thinking with study. As a fledgling theologian, I added layers of prayers and spiritual readings. At present, my wayward thoughts were because they linked my mother's obsessions to the cards and coincidences concurrent in my life. As a result, I had no choice but to analyze them, and there was an opportunity to do so.

---

*Professor Colman and Laurel are in mid-conversation.*

In a Zoom chat with Father Colman, for his Liturgy

course, I try to work out the dilemma of how to allay my mother's obsession through my confidence in their lack of a reality, which is, at the moment, neither a physical nor a mental possibility for me. The cards and coincidences prove that I am in some measure thinking about what she is. Basically, I want to know what overlaps between her and me that might be perceived as a threat to anyone. A term paper topic I talk about with Father is on the various assistant roles the priest has with him in the sanctuary during Mass. It is relevant to the course and my mother and I have shared in these roles. Without them, most parishioners wouldn't even know my mother and I existed.

"The Paschal Mystery is the center of our Catholic life and pastoral activity. Those who come to eat at the Supper of Our Lord, the body and blood consecrated by his ordained priests, are also called as his assistant deacons, altar servers, readers, and extraordinary ministers," my teacher reviews.

"Father, I never worried how I was perceived by the parish congregation at Mass whether in attendance or in the sanctuary. I'm who I am, you might say. Honestly, I worry that isn't good enough for some people lately, or might not have been so even in the past."

"There is nothing odd about that. People are warned by Our Lord not to judge, but they do. It's on them, not us. At Mass, the priest prays to God in the holy sanctuary. Since Vatican II, members of the laity trained in the assistant roles you mentioned are allowed purposefully in this space. There were years of discussion about it. The Council's reforms remain a challenge for some people and priests, as well."

"Father, I love that you're a priest and I'm not. I think people get that about me. But our differences seem to be getting in the way without my mother attending Mass with me

# The Body and Blood

regularly. Moreover, I think it got in the way even when she did. I just wasn't so aware of it, but through her intuition she was."

With our knowledge of one another through conversations and writings, he is privy of what I am experiencing at home and how that will direct my studies in his course.

"And yes, we have a topic. I like it. Give me a proposal."

"Catholic women in non-sacerdotal ministries during the Mass?"

"You're on track."

Father leaves time for us to talk longer, and he's satisfied this research will advance other papers and help me find my own answers. He has lifted me out of my problem and placed it in the realm of a theological inquiry. By the end of the semester, I have written a paper he recognizes as thinking that will allow me to remain committed and unafraid in my church ministries. My mother's obsession has stopped even though the pursuit continues.

The following week and the next, I bring her to the neurologist who says that her condition is unremarkable but he prescribes a mild medication. If I fill his prescription, the side effects are worse than the cure. I change her favorite TV shows from anything to do with violence and give her a low dose of Melatonin with improved results. A short time later, she receives a Mother's Day card from the Don, which I keep from her. Except for my own emotion, I am immune to both of them. I write a letter about the circumstantial and physical evidence, make three sets of copies for my attorney, the pastor, and the detective who was unable to solve Frank's case and put each correspondence in a manila envelope ready to be mailed. Depending on how I die, someone will be held accountable. The way out through a book seems the most plausible to me.

---

*Father John, and his sister Dr. Hannah.*

My emotional vulnerability is as palpable as the siblings' vulnerability. Except, they self-isolate and I am forced to. Separately, both of us are asked to receive counseling. When in college and later during the seminary, I took as many psychology courses as if a major in the subject. To self-diagnose my emotional state of mind, I waiver between anger and despair. As a diocesan priest, I am under the authority of the local bishop, and I submit to his power as well as protection over me. After returning from my visit to Poland, the tribunal overseeing my case pressures me to accept a full battery psychological evaluation. My Spiritual Director suggests that I enjoy the sights in the town I am scheduled for the appointment called Springfield, the capital of Illinois. I do, and report to the clinic in a positive frame of mind on a bright and sunny Monday morning.

"Father John, thank you for coming," says the psychologist. He is dressed in his white lab coat with the name Dr. Anderson printed over his heart. His outfit stays in my head in contrast to my Passionist priest friends, who wear a black cassock with the insignia 'Passion of Jesus Christ' over their hearts. Both represent groups of men with a different approach to people.

"Happy to comply. What's in store good doctor, a MMPI, Wechsler, Rorschach for starters?" I ask having studied these assessments thoroughly for school assignments.

"Oh, no Father, we are way past those in today's climate," he says menacingly, but I try not to read into his manner too much.

Nonetheless, the first day's tests include these plus a battery of others and physical examinations that extend into a five-day workup. If not for the text messages between my sister Hannah and me, and the time I spend sightseeing everything related to Abraham Lincoln, my compliance with the Bishop's request would have been harder.

"What are we doing today, Dr. Anderson?" I say, greeting him on the fifth day.

"Today, I will pass you over to Dr. Rogers. He conducts the qualitative analysis on surveys and interviews. Shall we?" he leads me to the next office down the hall and introduces me.

The first hour flies by. Then there is a day-long interview that breaks for lunch and ends early at 3:30. I am told that while the quantitative measurements are concluded, I will stay at the facility for another two weeks in individual and group therapeutic sessions with him and others.

Hannah is not respectable with that and texts, "Leave and I will back you up."

I do leave. I am fraught with conflict. Do I disobey my Bishop, who I dare not to? Or, do I obey a difference of opinion between psychologists, my sister who knows me for a lifetime, and a team who I met for five days? In a lengthy email I send to my Bishop, I explain the distress of my soul and beg for his mercy. Ultimately, I want nothing else than to obey the Will of God.

The drive home to Chicago is four hours and difficult on unfamiliar roads. By the last hour, it is late evening and dark.

Missing my exit, I pull onto the shoulder to back up. That's when I see the red lights and hear the sirens. I feel delivered from a worse fate.

# 10

# *Religious Coping Strategies*

*Father John. How practical self-care goals work.*

Nobody bothered me. I didn't receive the reprimand from the Bishop I expected nor a phone call from the Springfield clinic. However, I was given a moving violation from the police with a summons to appear in their local court in a month. Between my Spiritual Advisor and my sister, Hannah, I read the books and articles each suggest and keep the low profile they both recommend.

Ping.

"Hannah, good to see you, sis."

"How's my favorite priest? What are your thoughts?"

"Better, calmer, still upset about how I was ambushed," I give her emotional feedback she can read into.

"They need subjects. I guess the tests you took were enough to satisfy them. I'm sorry they probed about our family, about mama, you and us."

"That did get to me."

"The profession is under pressure to come up with explanations. Any sort of child abuse is emotionally damaging. Emanating from the clergy, it is a disorder no one can ignore. That's not you. You would be in a benign control group of priests suffering from displaced feelings of others. So, let's refocus. What did you think of the articles?"

"Significant. Your peer studies are valid. Priests are often isolated and overworked. Diocesans are the most public. On their good days and bad ones, they show up. They get the brunt. I also thought the article on coping mechanisms opened up ways for me to self-care. I wrote out a daily routine of personal goals. It's helpful. I haven't much else to do with myself. I miss being useful."

"These are just coping tools until you are reinstated. It's important to exercise and keep up."

"I'm in a small room, sis. It's not an Equinox Gym in here," I get her to laugh. "I've taken up painting."

"By numbers!" she teases back.

I'm grateful to have her company. With my computer in hand, I show her a canvas painting of the view from my window in acrylics and flip through a sketch pad of portraits in pastels. A life size terracotta sculpture of a dove with open wings, I have half-finished. We chat for about an hour which becomes a three-day weekly routine. The other two days I talk with my Spiritual Advisor for an hour over a virtual app.

*Father John. How spiritual readings coupled with prayers work.*

"What did you think of the book and website?" my Spiritual Advisor asks the question slightly differently than Hannah in his subject matter of theology.

"Sheen is always a good read, and the Catholic Bishops continue to outdo their website."

"And?"

"I'm interested in their pre-Cana links and stats. We

have much fewer divorces in Poland. US 50%, Poland 35%."

"Your parents have been married for how long, John?"

"Sixty-five years and all my siblings are married once," I feel so normal saying this.

"Once your case is over, maybe you would like to be a pre-Cana counselor?"

"Once this is over, I am going to be a tarnished priest."

"No, No, John. You are almost there. All the claims they leveled against you are either absolved or nearly so. Let's change the subject. What did you think about *Three to Get Married*?"

"Original for its time. Thinking of Sheen, I picked up an old habit of his I copied from *Treasure in Clay*. Between you and my sister, I have a filled-in sun up to down routine of secular and spiritual things to do. His hour meditation in front of the Sacred Heart is inspiring, I practice it between 11 and noon. Want to hear something interesting?"

"Please, go ahead."

"After my meditation I go to lunch. There is an old man I pass on my way in and out of the café who sits on his front stoop, which is directly across the street from church, so he knows where I am coming from. We nod politely for about a week, which escalates to a hello, and then to the weather. Yesterday, we had a conversation over lunch together. He's a fallen away Catholic since the broken marriage in his youth. I brought him to the pastor for confession and then we went to Mass this morning," I say with some amazement.

"So, your routine and meditation are working."

*Laurel. How theology studies and their application work.*

It is that time again. Time to register for the next course. Am I really taking another Master's degree at 70? Parish life is almost as difficult as working a regular job. There is a lot of misinformation out here about the rules of the Church. I am starting to be convinced that the number of Catholics would double if they understood the practicality and freedom religious values bring.

"What do you want to talk about first, your next course or how your book is coming along," my mentor graciously asks.

"My book, but it will determine which course, I hope."

"Where are you stuck?"

"Repentance."

"Penance is an early Church sacrament, and since placed after Baptism and before First Communion. Initially, the worst sins were announced in public," he says, raising an eyebrow. "Tertullian identifies three crushing sins: apostasy, murder, and adultery. Hermas writes about a father who neglects to chastise his sons sufficiently. Cyprian gives penance to the lapsed during persecution who return with a sincere heart. Ambrose advocates the gentleness of Christ to forgive rather than a revengeful, angry spirit. Augustine confesses his sins aloud and asks for understanding."

"Um, so I'm like Augustine asking God and my reader to help me understand why I ought to forgive others' sins pointed out by Tertullian. After all, sons are just like their fathers says Hermas; however, to be as gentle as Ambrose proposes will lead me closer to God and my faith community, giving sinners distance to repent and reform," I wince. "Sounds too hard to grasp in one course."

"You caught on to my analogy quickly enough. Besides, Early Church confessors included lay people with similar capabilities to yours, as well as, to priests."

"And this is why God sent me to you as my mentor. You have boundless confidence in me that I lack. How do I apply this information to contemporary situations where in my role as Eucharistic Minister, I give Communion to a penitent who killed my stepfather?"

"You are crushing it instead of examining it, Laurel. Take your foot off the snake and look at your situation from the outside. You are a minister of the celebrant. You are functioning on behalf of him and not the person who is coming to the altar to receive Communion with Christ. Everyone at the start of each Mass makes a public confession. This is theology not literature. You have to be careful what you fictionalize."

"Writing is the only way I will ever get over what happened to Frank. You're right, a hundred percent right. I have to stick to the subject matter, separate the sin from the sinner. This is easier said than done."

"I can register you for an Early Church history course," he states rather than asks.

"Is there any course that covers the Seal of Confession?" I have Father John in mind.

"Thirteenth Century. It grew out of private confession not to cause scandal. We are not offering a course for that period this semester."

Both of us stop talking.

"Laurel, I want you to think of something. Your book is fiction. You interpret the characters the way you want them to be, but you can't force their ending in real life. I can work with you to write a journal article instead. Set the book aside for a few more courses. Come back if you feel you're able to approach it then," he is sincere.

"Guess, that's the course. For the sake of wisdom or the prophet Job ending, I love Early Church History. I am satisfied with the choice."

---

*Father Mike. How the commitment to serve the people of God through priestly ministries work.*

I have prepared my thoughts for confession with Father Mark. This week so many little ones with their parents came for Reconciliation in preparation for the students' First Communion, that I had to examine my own conscience for weaknesses not to add to theirs. Besides addressing my sins, I have a plan for the topic of our evening meeting which is germane to those faults as well.

"Bless me Father for I have sinned. Lately, I have been diminished in my vocational goals. I think it is because I am too much in a comfort zone with the families I court. It's time to cultivate my societies and ministries more than I have and expand our parish activities."

"What's stopping you?" he asks, having turned our chairs in a perpendicular position for a reverent mood.

"Time is one, but involvement in parish societies is not my strong suit. I like to relate to families as a unit in their home. Church Societies are either men or women only."

"Why are you better at one and not the other?"

"It is at the heart of how I was raised. Family problems were aired around the dinner table, nightly. On Sundays, mom and dad cooked Italian with added courses for extended family who came. We would eat and talk for hours and hours. Everyone took a turn and everyone's problems were solved before they left. No male - female division. Just us."

"Sounds loving. All men or all women societies aren't?"

"Different. Distant. Cliques. More structure and prayers, less issue oriented."

"You say that you want to cultivate the parents of children with potential vocations. How can you parse out those you want, from those with other talents in your opinion?"

"Through parish activities, but this is my obstacle, my sin. It's time consuming. I am one person. Correction two now."

"Can you delegate the societies to your assistant?"

"Too new. He has to acclimate himself and the parishioners to him."

"Do you envision an approach other than working with the men and women societies separately?"

"Yes. Timewise, it requires that I bring them both together. Otherwise, I'm too rushed"

"And this is a problem, why?"

"The Societies are not families. They like being separated and distinct; they are smart enough to keep things that way. So instead of joining the men and women into one new society, I was thinking of a couple of Q&A sessions during the week to attract and define talents and contributions of those retired from those working."

"And this is a problem?"

"Small steps are hard for me. I envision the whole program."

"Um."

Again, I sense my weakness. "Patience. I am limited in the time it takes to implement the plan and impatient because to do it right takes time."

"Mike, you are honest, but the Lord has already given you what you ask. Combining the societies more than doubles your opportunity to realize your goal. With the topics parishioners pick and choose from, they will own the agenda and fill in the details themselves, along with your pastoral supervision."

And even though this is a confession and he deflects his full face from mine, I sense a look of agreement, as if saying this will make it happen. Still, I do feel the possibility. I feel able to leap out of the comfort zone of my family nest and into the area of delegating problem solving skills within groups and between heads of those groups with me around a parish council table. I am constantly amazed how brief and effective confession is for the soul.

Following through on my word, I invite a series of guest speakers, who are provided by the Office of the Bishop. A four-week afternoon and evening program open to the parish on relevant topics of faith held in our School Auditorium is held.

# 11

# *The Gerousia Plan*

*Father Mike. From words to deeds, out of his Comfort Zone.*

Tap, tap, the microphone on my lapel is on. Our school auditorium looks more than half-full with about 250. The digital clock above the entrance doorway reads 7:00. It is time.

"Hello Immaculate Conception Seniors! Welcome to the first meeting of Gerousia. I am delighted that all you fine people are inspired to come. We have a busy agenda for you this evening. I am going to use a PowerPoint presentation. So, let's start," I say, and after the sign of the cross and an invocation to the Blessed Virgin Mary, we do.

Clicking my computer device, the first slide appears on the big screen at center stage. "Our objective for this program is simply to renew our faith community. We want to rekindle the lives of seniors in a safe and independent parish environment, bring our families along with us on this journey, and initiate activities designed for each age group, in which to interact with one another" I click to show the next slide.

The picture is of a senior and adolescent sitting side-by-side at a dining room table peering into a computer laptop. "My staff and I will offer different ways you can access these slides and weekly updates online with a family or community member assisting you. For those who are tech savvy, the program has been posted on our parish webpage. Technology is just one way we shall use to bring the community inside your home which overall, we believe will astound you," and before I advance to the third slide, I place my clicker down to talk plainly.

"If you look around, you will see members of the Rosarian and Holy Name Societies, along with other ministries. Yes, we placed an open invitation to all parishioners in the bulletin, but we concentrated our efforts on the members I mentioned for two reasons. We want to strengthen the bonds within and between these groups, and we want you to be so pleased with this program that you invite others to join and increase this new endeavor to renew and foster parish life with you. There are no people better at doing this than you. You are the most hospitable in the parish. This is an easy statement to make and from my heart.

The title of this renewal program is Gerousia, a title that comes from the ancient Greeks. They were a committee of elders living in Sparta who reviewed laws and passed their judgments on them to the kings. You had to be 60 years old to be eligible. Raise your hand if you are at least 60," I strike a chord because nearly every hand in the room is raised, admitting to their age with gusto and yell out,

"Greetings, Gerousians!"

Sharing in their joyful commonality, I then resume the presentation and click to slide three, which displays a group of toga robed elders from that period. "They are you, back then," there is genuine laughter. These special elders are the people I want you to picture yourselves as. We are working from the top down to renew our mission of faith and expand your vision like rays of light. As seniors, you will concentrate on your faith and prayer life, as well as your relationships with teenagers, grandchildren, who you pass on your faith to. Each parish community is unique in this respect. Our elementary school is blessed in that we are over enrollment with an extensive waiting list. Our middle aged parishioners are occupied with an abundance of daily life activities. This is an older parish community with many founding members of our church who either live on their own or with their children. You are the influencers and sages; your family looks to you for stability and wisdom. When you are strong, they are strong, and as a faith filled community the Immaculate Conception parish is strong."

I work my enthusiasm up so that they feel it too, and after their applause I shift the approach of my presentation. "We have a short video that describes five activities we are prepared to put into action. As we advance, we will review more. Watch the presentation, and then rank your preference on the sheet with the pencils we placed in the center of your table. Next Wednesday, we will regroup back here at the same time. Bring a guest if you can. We will vote on which topics to prioritize and how to proceed from there. Sixty and seventy is the new middle age these days and eighty-year olds have vitality and ideas to challenge them. This is a community where our retirees want and have planned to stay in their homes until death do they part. Let's make that happen effortlessly and together as a faith-filled parish," stepping to the side, I click the video to play.

*Afterwards, with the list of 5 activities to rank in hand, the alt-group of six women sit together and agree to disagree on their importance.*

"This is a good deductible, Immaculate Conception School Scholarships," Ava writes 1 in that box.

"I tithe. That fits my purse this year," Sophie stresses this year with a grateful "Amen."

"You do know that you have to keep a correspondence

with the student you support?" Laurel reminds them.

"I don't do emails," Ava snaps back.

"We'll take them out to lunch. Correspondence doesn't have to mean an email. They can visit us and teach us the computer programs Father is talking about," Sophie interrupts.

"Actually, I think that is his idea: different talents with one goal. My first choice is school tutor. I do that already. I'll let one of my students set up my Facebook 'good morning and good night' page, Father suggested," says Rosa aloud, ranking her first choice.

"Mine is music or voice lessons. I'm thinking of one particular area of voice, public speaking. I would love to encourage young parishioners to read from the pulpit during Mass. With a new generation, we could work together to improve on our reading style if Father lets us," Claire says.

"That's a great way for young and old to cooperate. I can't think of anything I'm that good at," Sophie sounds disappointed.

"You're kidding us? It's right here, healthy lifestyle. You're a size seven your whole life. You eat and exercise without the slightest thought. It comes natural to you," Deanna wants her friend to acknowledge her assets.

"We could host the program together. I would focus on cooking and you on exercising. In return, the junior Gerousians could teach us new recipes and Tai Chi. I always wanted to learn that," Laurel says with hands that make an artful movement.

"Tai Chi is great for women our age. I'm making 'lifestyle' my number one pick," Deanna is eager, not having

# The Body and Blood

selected an activity to participate in yet.

"Good start. I like all these choices. I'm glad he's counting on seniors," Laurel says supportively.

"You know we all want to stay independent. Maybe, this would turn things around for the siblings?" Rosa waits.

"You think they were Father's inspiration for Gerousia? Wouldn't that be a divine plan?" Claire says, "You know, they are sitting at a table in the back."

"Guess they confessed and feel forgiven for damaging a priest's good name to show up," Ava grouses.

"They can't ruin his name, it's Father. They could discourage him in their persistent tempest," Sophie makes a thoughtful point.

"Ah! God is not in the storm, but in the still small voice that follows. Father John came to us as an ordained holy man, let's pray we haven't destroyed his vocation," Laurel says.

And without anyone thinking, they affirm their passion with an "Amen."

---

*Father John. The excommunication is lifted.*

There is a small private garden, at the rectory where I am staying. As often as I visit this garden no priestly company have I found. To amuse myself, I set up a bird -house and -bath and hang feeders in sturdy trees here and there. In imitation of St. Francis of Assisi, I share my pastoral conversations to the Lord in the presence of the one or many birds who listen. Today, there is a flock of birds chirping, but my heart is elsewhere in prayer. In my hands, I hold a letter from the

Bishop, which is likely to determine my fate as a priest. Before opening it, I bless myself and pray to be one with the decision. I read it aloud.

"To John, a holy priest,

During these past two years, your well-tried faith has shown me your resilience to endure a test of hearts for the people of God in place of yourself. Of those entrusted to me in the diocese and who I shared with you at the Immaculate Conception parish, two of my precious souls there had challenged your ability to shepherd them, and I had to remove you from their presence. Yet, you continued to obey my directives to refrain from any interference with our diocesan investigation and deferred to my access to your social media accounts. Further, you have shown yourself to be a true member of the body of Christ by following my instructions to refrain from any association with the siblings who brought charges against you: charges, of which you are now fully cleared. Within the month, you will receive your reassignment; however, I impress upon you to maintain no contact with them so as to allow the Spirit to work in their return to parish life.

In Christ, Bishop Lanciano."

"Did you hear that my little birds? Did you? My Savior has answered my prayers. I am overcome with joy. Amen."

---

*Laurel. Closure is an irresistible psychological and spiritual drive obtained through writing.*

With the draft of my book written, my mother's voice is an unspoken one that has to be addressed. Ever present in my thoughts are her pleadings, 'Promise me, Laurel, never even talk about this.' It is a voice like when you were a child and your parents and teachers explained why it is impolite to swear or use foul language and you had to test those words. Having worked with adolescents, sometimes those words were all I heard from them. Not to take it personally, I used to think of it as their way of exercising freedom of speech. What other power over frustrations did they have? Every semester for a fleeting two-minutes irrespective of the lesson material, a student went on a vulgar tirade. Besides writing a report to the social worker on the misbehavior, I would pause to explain to the whole class the etymology of the F-word. A police bastardized abbreviation "For Unlawful Carnal Knowledge." Regardless of their use of the word in the future, they would at least know that meaning and how other words might be more effective. That said, it was never that my mother's pleading made no sense, why I should not talk about what happened to Frank. I had to express my feelings, too, and for me freedom of the press was at stake. My mother yearned for closure and peace at the end of her life. I felt I was being given a way to help her with that.

What is more, it is terrible to be right, scared, and forbidden to express yourself. Since Frank went missing, a man in his 80s with everything to live for, my mother never even allowed my thoughts or words to dwell on the fact of what was so obvious to everyone around us. He was killed at the hands of the Mafia.

During the mourning period, a priest friend visited our house who was blunt. "They kill their own criminal types. Not someone like Frank," but adding barely audible, "evil."

I go back to the ninth commandment which is sad, because in the 35-years that my mother owned a business that thousands of local people sold their houses to others who brought them through her agency, each transaction was honest and ethically conducted. Of the hundreds of agents she employed, who earned commissions that enabled them to enjoy a lifestyle, she even empowered a few to compete with her and live the American dream of owning a small business. She was respected and acknowledged for her pioneering influence, and I grew to admire my mother in other ways than parenting.

"Mother, what if I knew the name of the person who killed Frank?" I ask her while watching a TV show that is relevant.

"What? Why are you talking about this again?"

The mere mention upsets her, and I tread lighter. "What if I wrote a book about a police murder investigation?"

"You are getting around the subject. Your name would be on the book. Promise me? Those who divulge their crimes are sought out with the revenge from them all."

Other than this topic, I enjoy her advice that comes to me on the level of parent to child, but there is something inside me that depends on her permission to publish my book. This is her story as well. "You don't realize it. You have been talking about Frank a lot lately, in front of my friends, your friends, your aides, even strangers. You say, 'he was such a good man, and how dare anyone harm and take him away'." I pause the TV.

"Once in a while," she admits sadly. "He was a decent, honorable man, who never hurt anyone. Don't get involved. He wouldn't want you to either. Frank was gentle," her memory of him is truly as he was.

"Am I not involved? Don't you think I loved him. Don't you know I hurt for him?"

"Laurel, you are the most precious gift God has given

me in the world. Nothing matters to me but you. Promise me, promise your mother. Never do anything to jeopardize your well-being. Frank would agree. They know no boundaries. They took a good man."

"I promise, but no one would harm me. I'm public."

"They do worse things or make it look like an accident. Promise your mother? I know."

Since Frank disappeared, she and I have left our opinion of who or why to ourselves. Still others in the neighborhood whom we haven't seen in a while ask, "Was your stepfather ever found?"

I think I would have let it be. I am almost positive I would have, if not for the pursuit. Since then, the question changed and centers on why a Don sends cards and plays cat and mouse with me after all these years. Despite this, I am front and center in the church. I am a daily communicant at the 9 alongside parishioners I call brothers and sisters, who are innocent in the crimes of their relatives long ago relocated or deceased. Another insight is my mother's recent calling out to God to know what happened to Frank, a mystery shared with others who wonder. All this resurrects the demise of Frank and a settling of accounts between men. As for me, how do I honor my promise to my mother and the wishes of my stepfather and still write my book, revealing the motive and name?

Understanding the question, I had no choice but to respect my mother's wishes. I would continue to talk about the theological aspects in graduate classes and write papers, as a way to gain understanding and to give reason to others if anything bad happened to me. Finally, I decided to include in my Will a codicil to publish my book posthumously under a pen name.

The truth has no time limit. My revelation of who killed Frank would be as meaningful in the near or distant future. God's will- not mine- be done.

# 12

# *Steadfast Love to God*

*Laurel's book gets published by mistake.*

The unthinkable happens.

"Yes, this is she," I answered the caller over the phone.

"This is Sandra Atlas from the Miller Literary Agency. We sent you a letter and numerous emails without any response. We decided to call," she says.

"Did you say The Miller Literary Agency?"

"Yes, Ms. Casey. We found your book, *The Pyx*, on Fiona. We are interested in developing it into a media format."

"Excuse me. Is my book published? Have you read it?" I am surprised further.

"Yes, of course. It is contemporary, conversational, convincing."

"It's online? *The Pyx*? Excuse me, Ms. Atlas, did you say?" I focus my thoughts.

"Call me Sandra."

"Sandra, may I have your number and I'll call you back. I have to check on something first." Disconnecting, I call my attorney.

"Helen Oakley, please, Laurel Casey," I wait and she

answers. "Helen, I just received a call from the Miller Literary Agency. A Ms. Atlas says they want to promote my book she found online. The one I told you was to be published posthumously. I'm not dead. Helen, this is a big problem."

"Collect yourself. Impossible. You wrote down your instructions, and you saw me place them in your file. I gave them to my secretary to type up and start the process of legalizing your pen name. Hold on, let me tell her to bring me your file." In the same breath, she puts me on hold.

The few minutes left hanging is a timeout to calm down to tranquil music.

"Laurel, I see what happened."

"What? What happened, Helen?"

"When we spoke, I heard you clearly say posthumous publication. Laurel, in your written instructions you left out posthumous. My office set up your past three books. After I signed off on your pen name documents, the secretary linked the book to your author page. Laurel, they are your written words. The firm is not culpable."

"Helen, I have to go. I'll talk with you when I digest this mess." I hear her say, "Okay, Laurel." We hang up equally peeved.

I yell out to God, "What am I going to do?" I'm thinking, the Church is going to excommunicate me, and the Mafia is going to kill me. I'm not just between a rock and a hard place. It is the definitive rock and hard place.

Whomever I would speak with or where ever I would go to think this over would all turn into petty distractions. In the quiet of my room, I pray. An hour later, I call Sandra. We make an appointment to meet at her midtown office, which starts with a marketing strategy to test the popularity of the book. In my codicil meeting with Helen, I left all the proceeds, if any, in an alumni scholarship pool. Heck, if I'm going to be dead over this, I might as well be altruistic. No doubt the diocesan Bishop will be upset about the negative press. There is always criticism in literature. I wrote a novel to help one priest and to celebrate another, and to honor a stepfather. I thought my mother was a lot to go up against, I am not about to take on the Catholic Church. Worried, I make an appointment with my mentor.

---

*Those who love God first shall find one another.*

Arriving on campus early to meet with him, I decide to make a visit to church. Sitting on the bench out front is the beloved Father Dara in prayer. The tall trees that shade him with the sound of birds chirping and the smell of the fresh cut lawn that fragrance the air, he is an idyllic picture of a peaceful man. As I approach, he holds up his rosary indicating he is on the last decade. We pray the mystery of the Institution of the Eucharist together. Finishing our courtesies, I become serious.

"Did you hear about my book, Father?" I say humbly.

"I have. It is in small print or I would have read it," he smiles.

"Do you think I'll be excommunicated?"

"They are afraid the nuns will want to be priests if the lay women usurp their position. Women are already doctors, lawyers, politicians, and Catholic novelists." He taps the top of my nose, instead of my hand, not a good sign.

"I am neither a wife, parent, nor family member to anyone besides my mother. I have been turned down by religious orders. I am aware of my surroundings and wrote about it. That is what writers do."

"You might have fictionalized your characters better. They are recognizable and fit your personal philosophy," his thought sounds prepared. "We're concerned the reader will be unable to separate the facts from your storytelling."

"I could defend myself, republish with someone's Afterword."

"Who taught you to be so clever?" he chuckles.

"I didn't want to write fiction, but I did want to communicate that the priests and the laity are united. Some on both sides are healing from the scandal."

"Yes, it is time to heal, isn't it?"

"There is a theological dimension to the book," I sound academic again, but can't take my words back.

"Rules are easy for you, Laurel. Obviously, not everyone can follow them. Who do you obey?" he asks a familiar question to my ears.

"I am not a loose cannon."

"In our circle, you are well-read by scholars who are persuaded by what you write, even if it were published posthumously."

"You know?"

"I've heard."

"You make a good argument," I admit. "That was for

my mother's benefit. I promised her."

"And what are you going to do about exposing the Mafia in your stepfather's disappearance?"

"No one should test whether I will overlook murder of a loved one in return for the Eucharist. I am faithful, but if I knew then what I know now, I would not have burdened myself with this ministry. The act left my mother and me vulnerable to what happened. My book is about theology and not about them."

"We realize that."

"Then why has this ministry done this to us?"

"It just happened, my child," he says, nodding sadly and diverting his eyes.

"This is too much to bear, Father."

"Oh Laurel. Your soul has become even more beautiful for the cross you carry. I am sorry it is so heavy at this moment." He places both hands on my head and prays, and afterwards he adds, "Stand your ground here. You wrote your book while enrolled in a Catholic university. You won't be excommunicated, but it might not be promoted in certain circles."

"Fair enough. Your blessing is special to me," I kiss his frail hand and leave confident. The meeting with my mentor works out as Father predicts.

---

*Laurel. Two men with the same background, one a nemesis and the other an ally.*

There is a weariness to God. God the Father waits impatiently for his children to return home, while the Son reapplies his charism to work through his chosen on earth to preach and administer his sacraments so their family will return home. God the Holy Spirit vies with the remnants of our original sin to choose their Trinity love instead of our self-will. In many ways, God is a teacher and a savior who speaks his words of wisdom and reveals them through our heart, soul, and mind. I hope there is more to His story for me. Sometimes I lose my way in his narrative.

This time I am certain of who he is. The old Don approaches the priest to receive the Host, and then turns to me, taking the chalice of the consecrated wine of the Most Precious Blood of Jesus Christ. Not that I wanted to give him the chalice; I cannot refuse. He's on a line. The nerve of him. When the Mass is over, I go into the sacristy to sign myself out on the attendance sheet and linger to check my thoughts. Leaving the church, it is empty but in the vestibule, I pass Sal holding his hand on the Wall for the Deceased. It is obvious: he has honored a loved one with a plaque and is praying.

I want to talk with somebody about what just happened, but do not think to disturb him. Except, he senses someone passing and looks, smiles and is consoled to share his thoughts, as well.

"My mom," he says simply.

"You miss her. You should. The child who takes care of their parents gives as much as the parent has given," I think about my own mother waiting for me at home.

"It's five years. She is with God and the angels."

"You were her blessing to the end. Sal, do you have a

The Body and Blood

few minutes to talk?" I'm on my way if he says no.

"Sure."

We go to sit comfortably at the grotto shrine.

"Please don't misunderstand me, but with your last name Coppola, you might be able to tell me why some people do the bad things they do. The man who I suspect murdered my stepdad came on the priest's line next to where I stood to offer communicants the consecrated wine of The Most Precious Blood. What does he want me to feel about him? Why does he pursue me?"

"Anybody who would hurt you commits a sin," he says protectively.

"Sal, tell me."

"They're *pazzo*. They have no shame. Don't think about them. It will get you in trouble. Think about God and his saints," he says and with his index and pinky fingers says some words in Italian.

"Sal that's not good enough for me. Everybody knows how to curse. Italians have a lot of style to theirs, but it is still cursing. I want to know his feelings. Either this man went to confession, received absolution, and legitimately is able to receive Communion or he mocks God and does so in the state of mortal sin. My real question is why does he insist on receiving the Eucharist from me?" I have no answer that would describe a normal emotion.

"They do go to confession for *malocchio* and think it will protect them against the people they harm. Their penance serves themselves. They never change," he blesses himself with the sign of the cross.

"Sal, stop it. I need to know," I chide him. He reminds me of the Italian side of my family, very animated in relating their emotions.

"He wants to fool himself, to think he has power over you because he believes there is a God. Without genuine repentant, he cannot be forgiven. He cannot take your stepfather's life without contrition."

"I get that, except the act, the sacrament, is too powerful to undermine. There is no way a sane person thinks God can be fooled. Then again, it is probably the way I think of insanity as variations of mental illnesses."

"*Madonna Mia*, protect her. He's *testa pazza*," his eyes look up to the heavens with prayerful hands.

"But what am I, what are we, if we allow him to do this and then distribute him Communion? What does that mean for me? He doesn't Confess to me? He doesn't do penance to heal my mother's psyche from her sorrow. While she is distraught over how this can and does happen, the murderer thrives. Are we fools, Sal?" admitting my helplessness over God is easy, but not over evil or crime.

"They're bastards," he looks up to the heavens again. "You're a saint. They are devils," and wipes his mouth with his fist.

"Sal, you're a saint. Don't be upset. God bless you and pray for us," I tap the top of his hand and leave to go home. Sal can't fathom it either, but his sincerity is enough for the moment.

A few weeks later, I receive a letter addressed from the man who is pursuing me. I debate with myself whether to just tear it up or open it. The chase has been going on too long.

Still, it may be evidence.

---

*Father John to be reassigned after the occasion of his first Mass.*

"Father Colman!" I called out. He is a few feet away in the midst of the crowd gathered outside church on Sunday morning.

"Laurel, you made it. He'll be happy to see you. He read your book. Well done." He gives a thumbs up. "I have a few minutes to vest. I'm his co-celebrant."

"I'll sit up front," and with that the priest, who has guided me through several courses and listened patiently to parts of the Father John saga, is gone. Today, he and I are here for that priest's first Mass reinstated in his visiting assignment in the parish of St. Stanislaus.

Bishop Lanciano is generous and has placed him in a predominantly Polish-American community. The church is one of the oldest in Chicago and named after a saint born and raised in Poland: Stanislaus Kostka. At the young age of 17, while studying as a novice for the Jesuit Order, he became ill and predicted his death on the Feast of the Immaculate Conception. By the will of God, he passed away as he lay in his bed surrounded by his fellow novices in prayers for him on August 15, 1568. The role model of a pious young seminarian, and all who respond to the call of a vocation in the Church, is important to celebrate and keep in mind. A calling to the Catholic priesthood starts out like any other interest a child growing up develops. Often, it is who nurtures the vocation that most influences the young boy. The discipline to the traditions come first and then, the commitment to one's trials for the faith follows. Different temptations perhaps, but not unlike any member of the faithful, a point often overlooked. When the seminarian studies culminate in Holy Orders, the vocation becomes divine. However, not every young man reaches his goal. Stanislaus did not because of ill health, but he, himself, was divine.

Watching Father John celebrate the Mass, I contemplate the long ordeal of this priest and in my Communion give thanks that God has kept him faithful to his vocation. At the conclusion, the pastor makes a brief announcement to those in attendance to introduce the visiting priest, whose smile and thank you wave show his genuine emotion. There is the expected applause and enthusiasm, but there is something more. I hear a smattering of this praise spoken in Polish. As Father makes his exit and stands outside the front doors of the church to greet his parishioners and accept their words of welcome, I wait. Last in line, he sees me.

"Laurel!"

"Father John," I skip the hand shake and go in for a hug.

"How did you know? I told no one."

"Father Colman. I spoke about you. When your assignment came through, he told me."

"Ah, he's the one who gave me your book. I spotted my character right away. Thank you," he gives gentle feedback.

"I imagine you have a busy afternoon. Am I allowed to call you?" I ask, having respected the Bishop's no contact wishes.

"Yes, we can speak. You've been doing that in your head with me anyway," his rosy cheeks fill out with a broad smile. "I have some time now?"

"Brunch? Lunch?"

"Neither. Come, we can talk in the priests' garden."

Walking with him, I realize how different my feelings are to the much older priests whose company I share. I have always felt protective of Father John, because he is the same nationality as my murdered stepfather, but he is also the age of a son.

"What a beautiful garden. The church has the best gardeners. Heavenly," I say thinking about a Bible passage following The Resurrection when a woman mistakes Christ for one. I close my eyes to imagine the natural fragrance of my environment.

"Do you hear them?"

At first I did not know what I was supposed to hear.

"Listen," he says softly.

"They're so happy," I am delighted by the chirping of birds. "They match my feelings."

"Sit here with me," Father escorts me to a white cement garden table with two benches. On his side, there is a knapsack from which he removes a copy of my book. "You gave me consolation. Finding myself as a character made me feel, once again, sent here and reconnected to a holy purpose. When I needed friends the most, I was alone without them or my family."

"I wasn't close to what happened but sensed something might go off between you and the siblings eventually. It wasn't until after you were removed that I learned of your differences.

The Bishop handled the situation the best way he thought, and that was pretty much the end. Not until the cards mailed to my house and the rest of the pursuit did I put together the pieces and see everybody else in a different light."

"It took me time to understand, but you were under their cloud too."

He acknowledges the reason for my marginalized treatment.

"How did you know I suffered your pain? It was one of the worst feelings I have had in my entire life. But still, I wasn't totally alone like you. Even with my mother in her condition, she was there for me," I say, admitting something I haven't revealed but to a handful of people. "Eventually, she wasn't enough and I reached out to an old mentor, to priests and faculty at my alma mater. Finally, I replaced Monsignor Luke with a new Spiritual Advisor. I regained my sense of safety with a different set of people."

"They won't ever stop, the naysayers and hypocrites," he sounds sad. "I am glad you were led in the right direction."

"You and I are stronger from our experiences. We know sin is an illusion to embrace and dispel for what it is rather than to fear and run away from. We endured what very few people can. We are both closer to God than we were before this started. You saved your priesthood, and I preserved what I went through for others to learn from."

"Melchizedek's Men," he gives a knowing wink to my other book.

"You belong to Christ for us. You're a good priest, Father. Culture got in your way. It could have been a different hyphenated culture than Italian-American. Criminal gangs are organized by all nationalities and races. But when crime is mixed with a religion, and atonement is left undone, it is the ill-conceived notion of criminals who are to blame. The religious know evil is the opposite of righteousness." I remind him. "For the next time, you will be cautious of a false sense of belonging as I am."

"Do you hear them?"

"The birds?" I nod.

"It was a very hard crisis of faith."

"Mine too. This was rare. I admit maybe coping alone is easier?"

"Your mother loves you. She's like mine."

"I imagine she is. Not many women are like them. God makes too few saints of married women, and less of divorced ones."

We chat a little longer, share what we didn't know about one another's experience. I talk about how I think my mom's recent obsession and prayers over Frank resulted in calling forth who killed him. He talks about his family in Poland and how they wanted him to stay home, but that he remained steadfast in his commitment to the Church in the United States.

"There are plenty of priests in Poland," he says reinforcing a commitment to us.

It had been almost two years since we spoke. He looked wiser in his mannerisms and at ease with himself. I was certain my reactions were not the only ripple effects from his presence at Immaculate Conception parish. In fact, Father mentioned a few parishioners who had defiantly remained in touch. I maintained a distant Facebook connection, but I could never stop thinking about the priest, a Polish man.

I believed at this very moment, Father John was sent by God to keep Frank's story alive for me. Like the church of St. Stanislaus Kostka, to which he was assigned and visited by a Polish priest and Cardinal, Karol Wojtyla, raised to a Pope and later canonized St. John Paul II, Father John hailed from a land and nation that demonstrated its mark on the History of the Catholic Church: Poland.

---

## Father Mike institutes Gerousia.

While nothing changed in my duties as pastor with respect to the existing ministries, societies, and organizations, I added an Outreach. I encouraged any man or woman 65 and older from all the other groups to join and help shape the Gerousia program. After my fourth Q&A, there were 150 seniors ready to join. Balancing this group with adolescents and young adults called juniors, we recruit older students from our elementary school students, plus Squires and Squirettes from the Knights of Columbus, and grandchildren of the Gerousians, and quickly reach the matching 150 juniors with extras placed on a waiting list. From both groups, I organize my council of four elected seniors and four juniors. With our mission established, and our agenda for the winter and spring completed, we are well underway.

Counted among the seniors are Mr. O and Mr. H, the President and Vice President of the Holy Name Society. They are also the fathers of the son and daughter who came out of the make-out room at the Confirmation party at Ildorato's. In one of those prayed - for miracles, both teens went on to attend the same college and an engagement looks hopeful.

## The Body and Blood

The pair of women elected come from the Rosarians and are friends who have been living on the same block since their children were born 40-some years ago. They are serious wives and mothers, but when sitting side-by-side they could make you laugh with tears just listening to their particular banter. In charge of the Annual Rosarian Christmas Party, Gina and Lucy raise consistently several times more than an entire year's contributions from all the societies combined. The duo is irreplaceable and perfect for the council. Like the Holy Name men, they know everyone in the neighborhood.

The four elected teens, also balanced in males and females, come from the KofC and our students' referred from our eighth graders. A Squire and a Squirette sent by the local chapter leader are recommended for their experience with at-home seniors and their planned college majors related to this field.

On the first Saturday of the month from 10 to noon, we meet in the rectory. What we decide here I review with my staff of professionals, but most ideas are approved, giving Gerousians' ownership to their society. This is our seventh council.

We start, as I do all my meetings, "In the name of the Father and of the Son and of the Holy Spirit. Amen." As usual, the topics for the agenda are open. We are at the stage of narrowing a seasonal range of programs. "Okay. How have you grown and developed Gerousia this past month?"

"I would like to start if I may?" Gina asks and receives no objection. "We are at the beginning of summer and teenagers who are off, without camp or a job to occupy their time need constructive activities. Lucy and I would like to advertise in the Church bulletin and online to conduct open rehearsals for a couple of plays. The plays themselves would

179

require a stage crew plus actors. Gerousians with interrelating skills would partner up with the teens to plan and carry out the production. We would sell tickets, of course," she winks at Lucy, jotting down a big US of one letter over the other.

As one council, all the members defer to me with no pretense. With this event, I ask the Holy Name how they might assist. Immediately, O and H offer free car service and help to build stage sets. The juniors suggest adding food with a matinee buffet and evening dinner theatre performance. Their project brings together teens and Gerousians, and we spend an hour of our meeting considering the obstacles and solutions.

"Mr. O, do you have something you want us to consider?" I ask after the Rosarians wrap up. I am hoping it is as good.

"We have an idea that pertains to the homebound in the parish. There is an increasing number. Your Eucharistic Ministers check on them and keep their spirit high, but from what we hear the homebound want more company," O passes around eight packets of five sheets of stapled papers which contain a proposal. "H and I have spoken with the Knights about coming into the parish to recruit teens for more Squires and Squirettes. They talked with us about an arrangement that might be of interest to the Gerousians. One of their Squirettes has been keeping a member's mom company for two hours after her school day for the past year. The member can't say enough of what a benefit the young girl is for his mom's state of mind, so he hired her. The girl looks after his mom on the weekends."

"I'm really happy for him, but how is that a charitable deed?"

"I hear you. In that it isn't, but it started out as one and remains partially so. The young girl comes from a family who attends Sunday Mass regularly. They believe in charity within their means and they encourage their daughter to do the same. She and the old woman play cards, look at her family pictures, write thank you notes, and bake cookies. The woman loves the company and didn't want to take advantage of her goodwill. Our member called the teen's parents. They all met. They cleared it with us, and the family hired the girl as a part-time aide. The Knights have no problem with it."

"How old is the teenager?"

"She is 16 and has working papers, Father. Our chapter accountant reviewed the employment and a member lawyer discussed the details with the old woman's family regarding insurance coverage. Not all homebound elders need extensive assistance: most just company. We could tie in how to use a virtual computer app where she would be in contact with others online. H and I see this as a way to build up the Squire program alongside Gerousia."

"I have to think about that. There is a big crossover between charity and payment," I am unconvinced, but I add, "I do know of a family who has done this, but the teenager is a next door neighbor."

In fact, there are many similar ideas that the council expresses in the Gerousia startup phase. At a general meeting, our 150 seniors agreed that the program ought to be a preparation for homecare and beyond. So, rather than ask who wants help with what, I invite guest speakers who are elder attorneys, health insurance brokers, and representatives from local funeral parlors. Parishioners are also invited to talk about other services: car rides, housecleaning, painters, handymen, and the like. Gerousian juniors show seniors how to order food and go shopping for all kinds of items online plus how to access companionship with parish societies for daily prayer and conversation, without leaving home if they prefer. Finally, the topic of sponsoring Catholics from other countries on work visas comes up. Live-in caretakers for parish residents able to provide a private apartment for the immigrant(s), they would sponsor to work for them. I could not help but think of how this brought the discussions between the siblings and Father John full-circle.

What was so wrong with the request from them? On the other hand, this fellow priest left his home and family to re-establish himself in the long process of becoming a citizen. Hurray for us. Father John brought from Poland his gift of the priesthood. We asked his Bishop; his didn't ask us or for ours. If America is to replenish her priestly vocations and we say that a newcomer is polluted in a short span of time, where else did he pick up his errant ways, if not from our culture, right?

Extending our meeting, we pray and reaffirm the purpose of our collective endeavor to nurture those who have a vocational calling. For all the effort I have been making among the married couples with children in my parish, reaching out for vocations through seniors who connect with juniors feels like one of the two best alternatives. The other is from the Sisters of Mother Teresa.

---

*Father Mike's year-in-review on vocations.*

The New Year will be here in a week and Father Mark has asked me to highlight two accomplishments of my pastoral work for the year. There are a few, but two trump them.

Starting with my first trip to the shelter, and not to underestimate the saintly groundwork laid by Mother Teresa and her sisters, the good deeds extended by Gene Lustig to two sheltered families bear fruit. In a year's time, the husbands and their wives each have employment, their children enrolled in parochial schools, and their home and well-being secured in a parish community. My sacramental service, begun through his penance to build up the Church from the bottom up, demonstrates I have put my words into actions not to suffer only wealthy parents, the calling of their children to serve the Church but the poor alike.

My second accomplishment is Gerousia. The parish seniors who are living the devout life of their faith. There is a special beauty to them, an indulgent look to their errors and those of others, a wisdom that remembers the truly good and a memory that disdains the bad, a softness around their frame. I was blessed with the best grandparents ever. I see them in every Gerousian man and woman. A pray for healing, the Outreach brings back the siblings to parish life and restores my priestly brother, Father John, to his ministry, and best for last has called-forth four seminarians and two women postulants.

Always ahead of me, my Spiritual Advisor has given me an assignment to treasure. God has indeed blessed me with an exceptional year.

# 13

# The Pyx

*Laurel. Something learned in elementary school.*

"Oh, the weather outside is frightful / But since we've no place to go / Let it snow, let it snow, let it snow," sings the crooner in his happy voice at volume ten.

"Alexa stop, stop. I do have a place to go and am awake," looking at Echo's face that confirms 7 AM, it is time to get up and start the day. With a quick look out the window, the forecast of snow covers everything for the season's first winter wonderland. Rarely do I change my routine that begins with daily Mass and certainly not today being Saturday, the day I bring the Holy Eucharist home from the priest for my mom. It is a perfect day and dressed in my snow clothes, I decide to enjoy the twenty-minute walk there and back: the time it takes to say my rosary.

Once outdoors, I am captured by the sense of being. I am enthralled by the sight. The snow white picture of a carless street with ice cycled trees vaulted over a silent drift that lifts the surface air ethereally. I remember a similar time walking in this same scene, when it was too dangerous to drive to a wedding where I was the maid-of-honor. Funny, I can picture the snow clearer in my mind than the wedding I attended. Nature. The contrast from yesterday's cold and clear weather makes me wonder if I am unappreciative of the beauty of a typical day. I put off the rosary as I am already enraptured in the exquisiteness of the divine.

There are five people at Mass including the priest, who invites the four of us into the sanctuary with him. Bob is his altar server, I am his reader and along with Ava and Sal, we recite the responses. There is a spirit of devotion to being old and attending Mass in this weather.

The walk back feels even more special with the sacred Host in my pyx tucked in a zipper compartment of my shoulder bag. As a woman, I take note of my surroundings but when carrying the substance of God plus walking alone I am alert. I don't have any such fear at the moment, the beauty of the weather absorbs me. Plus, when I arrive home, I will make the Communion ritual with my mom extra special by including her two aides to pray with us. The young women are Catholic who go to church on occasion. Regardless, I never push anyone to do anything and the choice to participate is fully theirs. My mom and I are ourselves, which means it is impossible for them to miss how much we love this sacrament together. That is why what happens, as I round the corner to my front door in a desolate part of the walk, challenges me rather than freezes me stiff.

"Laurel," the young man without a hat greets me.

"Louis," I shoot back. Surprised to see anyone, I shudder at how a familiar face is, regardless, a welcomed sight. He is the young seminarian I met in the pastor's office.

"I'm on my way to church. Is it open?"

"When I left after the 9, it was. Five of us," I say boasting.

"Troopers," he seems to have nothing more to say.

"Well, it's cold. Better keep moving," and am ready to take a step assuming he will say good-bye.

"My grandfather was given Last Rites yesterday," he blurts out instead.

"I'm so sorry, Louis. Were you close?"

"Very. There were two of us at his bedside, me and a priest. I overheard his confession. Among his many sins, he asked to be forgiven for killing your stepfather. My grandfather is Jimmy Stefano."

I can't believe what I am hearing. Without a word, I listen.

"He said that you helped his son, my dad, in that drug rehab you worked. Back then, your mother owned a business and he wanted her to make a deal she refused. You two were the first women to give out the Communion and read from the pulpit. You were taking the place of men. His manhood wasn't going to put up with it. He killed Frank, your man, to see how you would do without one. What do you think of that?"

"Your grandfather killed my stepdad? You heard him confess?"

"I said, I did. Who do you think you are? You women are taking over. My grandfather was right. Now, give me the Host?"

"What?"

"The Communion. You bring it home to your mother on Saturdays. Give it to me. You can't even be trusted to protect a piece of bread," he moves within inches.

"I don't have it."

"Give me your bag," he tugs at the shoulder strap.

## The Body and Blood

"Wait. I won't fight you. As a seminarian, I think of you as a holy person. Why is your grandfather's sin yours?"

"I just said. You were women who owned a business and didn't make deals he wanted. You were church ministers. Your family became his obsession."

"What will it prove if I give you the Host? What did it prove to your grandfather to receive it from my mother and me knowing he killed her husband and my stepfather? I have waited so long to know why."

"Oh, he confessed that too. You're nothing compared with his family's children and men. You're childless."

I unzip the compartment in my bag and remove the pyx. "Please don't make me do this. You are proving nothing, except that you and I are mortals. Don't you realize I forgive your grandfather, because on his deathbed I know he has confessed to killing a righteous man. There is no point in you repeating my frailty as a woman."

"Enough talk. Give me the Host of God," he says sarcastically and grabs my wrist.

I pull away. Carefully I open the small round wafer-size bejeweled container and expose the Host, hoping that the sight will change his heart, but there is no reaction. "Can we share the Communion?" I ask, hoping he will be consoled in his future confession of his sin. Truly, I believe this is a moment of insanity.

"Give me the Host or I'll take it."

I place the Host gently in his hand. Without adoring it, he brings the wafer to his mouth. Finished, he adds mocking me, "You can't protect anything" and leaves without another word spoken. He believes he has justified the reasons for his grandfather's rage.

There is a virtuous reason why this happened. There was no weapon or assault or even a threat to my life. It was completely an act of desecration. The man believed he had stolen the body of Christ from me, to prove I could not protect the Son of God. In a way that violated me as before; however, it was not the consecrated Host I gave him.

One day I had accidentally dropped the empty pyx and the medal disk inside came dislodged. Once in a while, I would obsess what would I do if anyone ever accosted me while carrying the Blessed Sacrament. Such vivid ideas were planted in my brain in elementary school by the nuns who taught us to protect the Holy Eucharist with our lives. So, I decided to use the space in back of the disk to place the consecrated Host and place a non-blessed wafer in the container. Thereafter, I never worried. My hypervigilant plan, that someone might do what was done to me, just happened. Thanks to heeding the nuns, I could protect Jesus! I go home and give the sacred Host to my mother. Except this Communion was extraordinary. I told her. She spoke about Frank peacefully, ever after.

---

*Parishioners celebrate Gerousia and new Vocations.*

Bishop Lanciano is the principal celebrant along with our pastor at our parish Mass to institute the Gerousia Society into the record. Sitting in the front row are the four seniors and four juniors installed as the first board of directors and across the aisle from them are four future seminarians and two young ladies for the novitiate.

After the Mass and the procession from the altar, Sophie

## The Body and Blood

says in a loud whisper to Ava that is overhead, "Isn't that amazing, six young people on their way to the religious life."

"And not all seminarians, but sisters up to the plate." Instead, Claire answers with robust.

"I thought the Bishop deferring to the accomplishments of Father Leonardi and Gerousia was gracious," Deanna sees another dimension.

"The Bishop's homily was inspirational," Rosa leans in smiling.

"To have the Bishop acknowledge our pastor and parish work and prayers that went into these vocations and outreach to our seniors, this Mass was indeed extraordinary," I say to include their points-of-view.

As we leave with these uplifting thoughts, we blend in with the congregation, walk out the front doors and over to the school for the wine and cheese celebration. Reaching in my shoulder bag to put on my sunglasses, I realize I have left them in church and run back. There in the third pew, staring me in the face are my missing glasses. I am captivated for a moment. The sacristan has already turned off the lights, except for the one over the sanctuary. There is something inviting to be alone with God in his house. I knee in prayer and then think to light a candle to St. Anthony, at the back of the church where his statue is.

"St. Anthony, thank you for helping me find my sunglasses." Feeling it is too bland, my head turns towards another statute, the Pieta. I am overcome.

"Dear Virgin Mary and Our Savior, I haven't beheld you in my eyes this way for a while. I see in you a unity and a bond of love and compassion for humanity beyond the norm. Only through knowledge of your death and resurrection, Jesus, could I be given closure on Frank's murder and enlightenment of it through your Holy Spirit. Only through the purity of a Mother and child's love for one another can I understand the meaning of human life and others' desire for eternal life. With this in mind, I make a special prayer. It is about Louis.

He missed the ceremony, and I heard he dropped out of the seminary. Father Leonardi made him apologize, and I did keep the Host for my mother. Besides, his grandfather rallied after Extreme Unction, so might you use his penance to change his grandson? Louis knew his grandfather as a man he loved and who cared about him. He just can't love him more than God and those who love God back. I can't speak for Frank or my mother, but I think I know them well enough, so that I might. Louis made a mistake in judgment."

Ending my prayer, I make the sign of the cross on myself and am ready to leave for the social, when I overhear and turn to see Father Leonardi at the foot of the sanctuary begin to pray aloud. He stands with arms outstretched and is reminiscent of our former pastor.

"Father, I thank you for my people."

# *Epilogue*

"Did you like the ending?" I turn to my guest.

"Peter, I am overwhelmed, lost for words," Frank says honestly.

"Personally, I thought your story would never get told, but your stepdaughter persevered, a real truth seeker with a byline written with the hand of God."

"It hurt her to face the reality of how I died. So many people protected her from these thoughts, none more than her mother and our priest friends."

"You were a good man in your lifetime. Why shouldn't she talk you up? We didn't like it one iota up here when you were murdered and the aftermath, with their taking Communion from your wife and her to rub in who they think they are. That really upset us. The Holy Spirit had to work in his own fashion for this revelation and truth to come out. Prayers, deeds, books, we like all these endings. Laurel is in a circle of holy men and women. We made certain of that. Come, let me show you around," I tap the top of his hand and the two of us get up and with a lively stride walk together through the narrow and pearly Gates of Heaven.

Made in the USA
Middletown, DE
29 September 2023